STRANGE SOUNDS...

At one fifteen, Kate came awake with a start. She lay blinking up at the ceiling, wondering where she was. After a moment, she remembered. Something had awakened her, but she didn't know what. Probably a fridge motor kicking on, or a settling in the walls—strange house, strange noises. Nothing to worry about.

Then she heard it again, a sound so faint she wondered if she was imagining it. Before she knew it, she was on her feet and peering out the window. Nothing but darkness out there. She could hear the waters of Lake Winnipeg lapping at the shore and the croaking of frogs somewhere nearby.

It had sounded like a woman crying.

THE WEEPING WOMAN

by

MARCELLE DUBÉ

FALCON
RIDGE
PUBLISHING

For Linda Garson, who always believed.

My thanks to Irene Marks for her endless patience with my endless questions. I hope she will forgive the liberties I took with her town.

THEWEEPINGWOMAN

by

MARCELLE DUBÉ

CHAPTER 1

KATE DROVE slowly, peering into the darkness outside her Explorer. Maybe she had already passed number twelve. She hadn't seen a barrel filled with flowers, but she could easily have missed it with no streetlights and only her headlights to guide her. Still, she didn't think she'd gone past it— she was sure she'd seen Number Four on a post about half a kilometer back.

Served her right for leaving the station so late. Amanda had warned her to come while it was still light.

"It's tricky to find," she'd said over the phone. "But the view is worth it."

Well, there was no view now, except for the occasional porch light down a narrow driveway or the glimmer of moonlight on water glimpsed through the trees. She had powered down the passenger window because it reflected the dashboard lights and her own ghostly image. Now the Manitoba summer night filled the Explorer, rich with the smell of damp earth, freshly-mown grass, and sweet clover. Every time she slowed down to check the number on a cottage, the sounds of crickets threatened to overpower the quiet purring of the engine.

The two-and-a-half-hour drive from Mendenhall had given her time to review the instructions she had left with Deputy Chief

McKell. She didn't think she had forgotten anything, but she had promised the DC she would check in regularly.

She was pretty sure he'd rolled his eyes when her back was turned.

Kate gritted her teeth and kept staring into the night. *You're doing this for Amanda,* she reminded herself.

She was worried about the girl. Her niece had started her catering business barely a month after getting shot. She should have gone home to Montreal, where Rose and John, her parents, could have looked after her, but she had insisted on staying in Mendenhall with Kate. Kate had done her best, and physically, Amanda seemed to have recovered well, but lately she had begun to look... strained. She had grown thinner, and there were dark circles under her eyes.

It had been Kate's idea to get away for a week. Maybe walking the trails and hanging out by the beach would give Amanda time to herself, time to rest—

Her foot found the brake a second before her eyes recognized that she was looking at a large wooden barrel with red and yellow nasturtiums spilling from it. The large number twelve in white on the barrel also helped. She backed up until she came abreast of the driveway and turned in. To her surprise, the driveway ended within a hundred feet at an old-fashioned stand-alone garage with large barn doors. Amanda's green Tercel was parked in front.

To the right of the garage stood the cottage, hidden by a thick screen of trees until she turned into the driveway. The web site had cited four bedrooms, an eat-in kitchen, a living room, one bathroom, and a screened-in porch. There were two windows on the side of the house facing the driveway. One was dark, but a soft glow came from the other window, as if somewhere deep inside the house a light was on. Another light burned above the front door but it, too, had been hidden by the trees.

Relieved, Kate pulled up next to the Tercel and turned the engine off. Then she turned the key again to roll up the window.

Finally, she emerged from the Explorer and stood enjoying the quiet.

There were no street lights here. No traffic. It was just past nine p.m. and there were no shrieks of kids in the lake, no sounds of motorboats racing, no loud music. Quiet.

It wouldn't last.

The cottage was about a mile north of Gimli, the small Icelandic community on Lake Winnipeg. Everyone from her Mendenhall deputy chief, Rob McKell, to Bert in Winnipeg had recommended Gimli as a great getaway. She stared at the quiet house.

It'll be fun, she told herself. *Really.*

She hadn't been to a cottage since she was a kid growing up in Quebec's Eastern Townships, but she remembered long lazy days of swimming and lying around doing nothing. She hoped she'd survive it.

She reached into the back seat for her bag and turned toward the front of the house. Then her gaze swept past the roofline and she craned her head back to look at the stars. She blinked in surprise. Where had they all come from? She'd been so busy driving and thinking that she'd paid no mind to the night sky. Obeying a sudden impulse, she set the bag down on the driveway and took the stone path between the garage and the back of the house. It led her to a set of stairs and a darkened, screened-in porch.

A breeze fluttered the short sleeves of her cotton shirt and sent goose bumps chasing each other up her arms. It was cooler than she had expected for June. The scent of roses teased her but she couldn't tell where it came from.

There were no lights at the back of the house, but between the crescent moon and the starlight, she saw enough to distinguish a small garden shed on the far side of the house and some kind of table deeper into the grounds. She left the path and found herself walking on luxuriously thick and springy grass that needed cutting.

Then she heard the lapping of water and blinked. Of course.

The cottage was on the shore of Lake Winnipeg. According to Bert, the deputy chief of the Winnipeg Police Service and her lover, it was one of the largest inland lakes in the world. She drew closer to the table and saw that it was one of those round ones with an umbrella planted in the middle. It must be a lovely view during the day. The web site said something about a canoe and a dock, but she'd have to wait until morning to look for them. And she wasn't sure how she felt about taking a canoe out on a lake that was so big it should have tides.

A mosquito found the exposed flesh of her neck and she swatted it away. Maybe it was cool because of the proximity of the lake. It was certainly much warmer in Mendenhall.

A movement caught the corner of her eye and she turned. Where the garage ended, a hedge of tall pine trees acted as a privacy screen between this cottage and the one next door. As the wind picked up and the branches swayed, she thought she caught sight of a moving light. There was someone in the yard next door.

But as she watched, the light seemed to climb higher and higher, finally stopping at what she guessed was the second floor. There must be an outside stairway leading to the second floor.

She stepped closer to the trees, trying to make out the shape of the cottage next door.

"Careful, Aunt Kate."

Kate jumped and whirled at the same time and lost her balance. Arms flailing, she tried to recover, but her foot slipped. She had time to gasp in alarm as she suddenly sensed emptiness below her, then a strong hand grabbed her shirt and hauled her away from the edge.

"Are you all right?" asked Amanda, transferring her grip from the thin cotton shirt to Kate's arms.

Kate looked back over her shoulder and blinked. Holy cow. The grassed yard gave way here to a beach gleaming dully ten feet below. Now that she knew what she was looking at, she could see how the long grasses disguised the drop off.

"Why isn't there a fence?" she asked, still shaking from her close call. It was only a ten-foot drop, and the landing would have been on sand, but still...

"I don't know," said Amanda. "Maybe because it would obstruct the view. This wouldn't be a good place for kids."

Or middle-aged chiefs of police, apparently. Kate gave her niece a quick hug. Amanda's blond hair gleamed palely in the moonlight.

"Sorry I'm so late, sweetie," she said. "I had trouble getting away from the station."

"I know," said Amanda, and Kate could hear the grin in her voice.

"And how would you know?" asked Kate suspiciously.

Amanda took Kate's hand and started pulling her toward the house. "Oh, I have my sources," she said airily.

I'll just bet.

Amanda had arrived in Mendenhall in the middle of the coldest February in recent Manitoba history. Despite getting shot by a madwoman, she had fallen under the spell of the Prairies and decided to stay with Kate for a while. It had worked out surprisingly well, despite the small size of Kate's house.

The entire Mendenhall Police Department—all seventeen constables plus Charlotte, the station's only admin person—seemed to have adopted Amanda. And fifteen of the sixteen male constables seemed to have a bit of a crush on her, all except for Deputy Chief Rob McKell, who treated her more like a daughter. And Marco Trepalli, Kate's youngest constable, was now officially dating Amanda.

Kate sighed.

"Where's your suitcase?" asked Amanda when they reached the stone path.

"Hang on," said Kate. She retrieved her bag from the driveway and followed Amanda up the stairs that led to the screened in porch. Amanda opened the screen door and went inside. A second later, a light flickered on.

"Don't let the bugs in," said Amanda as Kate dawdled in the doorway.

Kate stepped inside and let the door slap her on the bum. She reached behind her and pulled it closed. At the far end of the porch, a round table with four chairs accommodated card players or *al fresco* meals. At the near end, a wicker couch sat back against the inside brick wall, looking out at the dark yard. A matching wicker coffee table sat in front of it, flanked by two petite chairs with thick, flowery cushions for seats.

"Are you hungry?" asked Amanda. "I've got a nice salad or some cold chicken."

Of course she did. When did Amanda *not* have food ready? Kate queried her stomach, which informed her that yes, she could eat something, but no, she wasn't really hungry.

"Maybe just something to drink," said Kate, following her niece through the inside door just past the couch. She smiled to herself at Amanda's proprietary air. They had planned to travel together, but Kate had gotten caught up at the station and Amanda had decided to go on ahead.

Amanda turned on another light and Kate found herself in the kitchen. It was larger than she had expected from the pictures. No granite counter tops, but the yellow walls were cheerful and the black and white tiles on the floor reminded her of her first apartment. Another table waited in here, also round, with four wooden chairs, all mismatched. Kate liked it.

"It's not big," said Amanda, "but it'll do. Two of the bedrooms face the road, and two face the lake. I picked one of the lake rooms." She led the way to a hallway. Kate had a glimpse of a darkened living room just off the kitchen and then Amanda pointed down the hall, to the right.

"That's the biggest bedroom," she said. She waved at the direction of the outside door. "Front door." She marched down the hallway. "Bathroom." She waved to the right. "Second bedroom." It was on the same side as the bathroom. She backtracked a few feet and waved to the left.

"My room," she said, leaning in to flick on the lights.

"Very rustic," murmured Kate, noting the wood-paneled walls and plaid wool blanket.

"And you could take this one," said Amanda, opening the door to the far room. She turned on the light and stepped inside.

"That's a brass bed," said Kate, eyeing the double bed with its bright yellow and green quilt.

Amanda grinned. "I knew you'd like it," she said. "And look at the trunk! It's got to be nearly a hundred years old!"

Kate smiled. The room was fine. A dresser, a small closet. She dropped her bag on the trunk at the foot of the bed, ignoring Amanda's sharp intake of breath, and walked over to the window. She opened it and immediately the breeze fluttered the gauzy blue curtains. There were blinds, too, for those who wanted to sleep in. And a screen on the window.

"This will do nicely," she said with satisfaction.

"I'm so glad we decided to do this!" said Amanda. "We can go canoeing and hiking, and we can explore Gimli—did you know they have a harbor?"

While Amanda prattled on, Kate began to unpack. This *was* a good idea, after all, judging by Amanda's enthusiasm.

And a week of rest by the water... No paperwork, no constables, no McKell... It would do her good, too, to take a break from the station.

She grinned to herself. And it would do the station good to get a break from *her*.

* * *

At one fifteen, Kate came awake with a start. She lay blinking up at the ceiling, wondering where she was. After a moment, she remembered. Something had awakened her, but she didn't know what. Probably a fridge motor kicking on, or a settling in the walls—strange house, strange noises. Nothing to worry about.

Then she heard it again, a sound so faint she wondered if she was imagining it. Before she knew it, she was on her feet and peering out the window. Nothing but darkness out there. She could hear the waters of Lake Winnipeg lapping at the shore and the croaking of frogs somewhere nearby.

It had sounded like a woman crying.

She plucked her sweatshirt off the foot of the bed and pulled it over her thin pyjamas, then padded to the door and opened it quietly. No sound from Amanda's room. Good.

She made her way down the hallway and into the kitchen. Peering through the window over the sink, she saw only darkness with a hint of movement from the swaying pine trees beyond the garage.

This was silly. It was the middle of the night. The wind sighing through the trees had woken her up and now she was imagining things.

But she wouldn't get any more sleep until she was sure there was no one out there. With a sigh, she opened the kitchen door and stepped onto the porch. The floor felt warm against her bare feet as the wooden planks gave up the heat of the day, but the night air was cool. She pushed open the screen door and walked down the steps to the stone flagging, and immediately her toes curled in protest. The stones were definitely colder than the porch floor.

The lawn felt lush and cool. Fortunately, there was no dew yet. She walked to the middle of the back yard and stopped to listen. The long seconds ticked by as she sorted through the sounds. Water on sand. The soft, rhythmic thumping of wood on wood—a boat against a dock? An owl somewhere to her right. The plaintive meow of a cat.

There! The faint sound of crying reached her straining ears, carried by the breeze, and she automatically turned toward it. It was coming from next door, where she'd seen the light earlier. Moving swiftly to the pine trees, she pushed apart the boughs and peered into the darkness of the neighboring yard.

"Hello?" she called softly. "Are you all right?"

As she waited for a response, she slowly became aware that someone was there in the inky darkness, just beyond the trees.

"Are you hurt?" she whispered. "Can I help you?" She had no idea why she was whispering except that she had the sense the woman had been muffling her cries. Maybe she had come outside to cry because she didn't want whoever was inside to hear her.

Then the light appeared again and slowly made its way up, as if whoever held it was climbing to the second floor. She waited a few more minutes but heard nothing else. Whoever had been out there, crying, had gone inside.

Good idea, she decided as she began to shiver.

It's late, it's cold, and you're tired. Go to bed.

So she did, but it was a long time before she fell asleep, and when she did, she was still listening for the faint sound of weeping.

CHAPTER 2

AMANDA HAD the coffee going by the time Kate yawned her way into the kitchen. Sunlight poured into the room, catching in Amanda's blond hair, which fell loose to her shoulders, thick and honey colored. She wore flannel pyjama bottoms and a bright red hoodie over a tee-shirt that Kate suspected belonged to Trepalli.

"Good morning," said Amanda cheerfully when Kate walked in. "Coffee?"

"Your parents did a good job with you," said Kate, accepting the mug. She considered sitting out on the porch, but one glance outside at the dew-covered lawn convinced her that it was probably a little chilly. She pulled back a chair from the round table and sat down before taking a sip. Good girl. She had remembered the sugar.

"The fresh air must agree with you," said Amanda as she poured herself a cup. "You *never* sleep in."

Kate raised an eyebrow. Mendenhall air was fresh and clean, too. Well, except for when the wind blew from the south, carrying the aroma of Connelly's pig farm.

"I didn't sleep in," Kate pointed out. "*You* are up unnaturally early." In fact, the dark circles under Amanda's eyes looked even darker today than they had yesterday. What was the point of leaving Mendenhall only to *not* sleep in Gimli?

Kate fished her cell phone out of her jean pocket and began dialing the number for the Mendenhall Police Department. Amanda glanced over her shoulder and frowned. She set her mug down on the counter, marched over to Kate, and plucked the phone out of her hands.

"No calling the station," she said firmly.

Kate stared at the phone in Amanda's hands. Taking a holiday was one thing, but she wasn't even allowed to call?

"I just want to check in," said Kate, reaching for the phone.

"No." Amanda retreated a few feet and placed the cell phone on top of the refrigerator. "They can call you if they need you."

That was true. McKell would call if he needed her. Say, for instance, when an asteroid was on a collision course with Mendenhall.

She watched Amanda open the refrigerator door and peer inside.

"I thought maybe an omelet this morning," said Amanda musingly, almost to herself. "I have feta and spinach, and some nice sourdough bread. Or would you rather have pancakes? I've got cranberries and chocolate chips."

Kate tried to remember what her breakfasts had been like before her niece arrived. Bagels, she thought. Maybe oatmeal, sometimes. Amanda had been a sous-chef at a fine Montreal restaurant before moving to Mendenhall. Kate still couldn't figure out why the girl had decided to stay. Trepalli, probably.

She wasn't sure her sister Rose would ever forgive her.

"An omelet sounds lovely," said Kate, getting up to help. "By the way, have you met our neighbors?"

Amanda handed her the carton of eggs and a tub of feta cheese. "No. I got here at dinnertime, and by the time I had finished unloading the food and checking out the dock, it was getting dark. I made dinner and read while I waited for you. Why do you ask?"

Kate opened one cupboard door after another, looking for a

bowl, and finally found them in one of the deep drawers next to the dishwasher. This was *so* not like the cottages of her youth.

"I thought I heard someone crying last night," said Kate, putting a bowl on the counter. She pulled open a drawer, looking for a whisk. "I went out there but didn't see anyone."

Amanda had pulled four eggs from the carton and now stood staring at Kate, two eggs in each hand. Her blue eyes looked troubled.

"I thought I dreamed it," she said slowly. "A woman, crying, as if…" She paused, then shrugged and set the eggs down on the cutting board next to the bowl. "I don't know like what. In my dream, though, it was me crying."

A shiver ran up Kate's scalp but she smiled reassuringly at her niece. "Nothing like a strange bed in a strange place, eh?"

Amanda shrugged. "I guess." She broke the eggs into the bowl and Kate found a frying pan large enough to accommodate the omelet. It wasn't her imagination, then, if the sound had wound itself into Amanda's dreams. Disquieted, Kate decided she might just nose around after breakfast.

"So," she said finally, when the silence had stretched on uncomfortably. "What did you find at the dock?"

Amanda brightened immediately. "There's a canoe," she said. "I haven't used a canoe since Mom and Dad used to take us camping. Remember?"

Oh yes, she remembered. For a while there, every time Kate returned to Montreal for a visit, Rose and John would pack up Amanda and her brother Sean and take everyone camping. They all seemed to enjoy it, but as far as Kate was concerned, her ancestors had worked long and hard so that she could have electricity and running water and wouldn't have to cook over an open fire.

Still, the whole reason she was here was to give Amanda a bit of a holiday. If Amanda wanted to go canoeing, then Kate would take her canoeing.

"It's been a while for me, too," she warned her niece.

But Amanda just waved away the objection. "Nonsense," she said. "It's like riding a bike."

* * *

The "bike" kept trying to drown her.

"No," said Amanda patiently. "Aunt Kate, just sit down on the edge of the dock and put your feet in first."

This was embarrassing. Kate stood on the dock and stared at the canoe. It was low, like some kind of sports car that you fell into and needed to be hauled out of. Amanda had demonstrated how easy it was to get in and out. Twice. But Kate just couldn't get past the image of her with one foot in the canoe and the other on the dock, and the canoe slowly drifting away from the dock.

The dock needed a ladder, she finally decided as she lowered herself to a sitting position. Amanda sat in the stern and held on to one of the log uprights that supported the dock.

"That's it," said Amanda encouragingly. "Now lower yourself into the center of the canoe."

Just do it, Kate told herself sternly. *For Pete's sake, you've taken down killers. You've been* shot at. *You can handle a canoe.*

She took a deep breath and lowered her feet the six inches to the bottom of the canoe, then hauled her bum off the dock to a crouching position in the middle of the canoe. Both canoe and bum wobbled dangerously.

"Good," said Amanda behind her. "Now hang on to the dock for stability and go up to the bow seat."

Kate worked her shaky way up to the front seat and carefully raised one leg after the other so she could end up facing the right way when she sat down. The canoe rocked as the waves gently rolled to shore. Surely getting into a canoe hadn't always been so tricky?

But once her bum was safely on the woven seat, she found herself looking around with pleasure. Their cottage was on a small point, so that the cottages to the north were out of sight. From her vantage point, she could see where the lawn ended abruptly at a ten-foot embankment. The steps leading to the dock were made out of rounded stones and the handrail consisted of driftwood. She could see the roof, part of the porch, and the back wall of the cottage, which was painted a pale green with white trim. She couldn't see the flower garden with its rose bushes at either end, but to her right, the screen of pines hid the neighboring cottage, which occupied the point with hers.

"Ready?" asked Amanda behind her.

"Ready," said Kate. She reached down and pulled the paddle out from under the seat, then glanced over her shoulder. Amanda had her paddle already in the water. Kate put hers in the same side and together they stroked. The canoe, a bright red fiberglass thing with the name "Nellie" painted in white at the bow, slowly began to turn. When it finally faced the lake, Kate switched sides so they wouldn't continue to go in circles.

At once, the sheer size of the lake gave her pause. Holy cow. It might as well be an *ocean*! What were they *doing*?

But Amanda's paddle dipped, stroked, and emerged regularly, as if the girl had no worries. Kate wasn't about to admit fear, so she matched the girl's strokes and the canoe surged forward, slightly angled against the waves.

In silent agreement, they headed north, past the screen of pines. Clearly, Amanda was as curious as she was about their neighbors. It was slow going, but they stayed close to the shore and eventually rounded the point.

The neighboring "cottage" was a two-storey house with peeling white clapboard siding and a cedar shingle roof. It was set back from the shore about a hundred feet, but from her vantage point, Kate could see that the yard was overgrown and the house in need of a fresh coat of paint. There was a balcony on the second floor, which acted as a roof for the porch, and a small, one-storey extension on the north side of the building. Probably the summer kitchen. A wall of stones, set into the earth, separated lawn from beach, clearly an effort to prevent further erosion. Some of the stones had fallen out and either lay where they had fallen or had been carried away by past storms. A boulder half her height sat on the sand in front of the pine trees and acted as a natural separation between the two beaches.

The place looked like it had been abandoned for years.

"There's someone watching us," said Amanda.

Kate looked back at her but Amanda was watching the house. Kate glanced back but there was no one on the porch. Then she spotted the twitching curtain at the window and realized that Amanda was right.

"Maybe it's the crazy aunt," teased Amanda, "locked in the attic, away from people."

"You read too many gothics," said Kate. Besides, the curious watcher had been on the main floor.

They kept paddling and rounded the point, where the wind caught them and immediately fought them for every gained inch.

Amanda laughed and paddled harder and Kate remembered why she hadn't kept up her canoeing when blisters began to form in the palm of her hand.

Beyond the point, the shore swept into a deep half-moon of pale sandy beach gradually climbing and merging into shallow yards. Where their cottage was on a respectable piece of land, most of the cottages in the tiny bay huddled close together, barely kept apart by hedges or screens of trees. The cottages were smaller, but newer.

Everywhere she looked, children ran in and out of doors or played at the edge of the water, even though it had to be cool. A body of water the size of Lake Winnipeg would take a while to warm up in summer. Two younger kids were working industriously at making a sand castle. At least, she thought it was a sand castle.

Even from this distance, she could hear the calls of parents and the shrieks of children.

"Shall we go back?" asked Amanda. "I brought chocolate chip banana muffins."

Kate agreed out loud that it was probably enough for a first time out, while privately promising herself not to do this again. They turned the canoe around, and with the help of the wind, rounded the spit of land quickly.

"Look, Aunt Kate," said Amanda. "There's someone on the porch now."

Kate looked up at their neighboring cottage and sure enough, someone was standing on the porch, at the top of the stairs leading to the lawn. A woman, dressed in a white, long-sleeved shirt and a pair of loose pants. Maybe it was a long skirt. Hard to tell at this distance.

Was that the woman she had heard crying last night?

Impulsively, she pulled the paddle out of the water and rested it on the gunwale, then waved at the woman. The woman just stared at them and made no move to wave back. It was hard to make out her features.

"So much for friendly neighbors," said Amanda.

Kate picked up the paddle and dipped it back in the water.

* * *

After lunch, they drove to Gimli. They walked along the sun-splashed boardwalk, admiring the endless expanse of Lake Winnipeg. Waves washed up on shore, as if enticing the children on the beach to come play. The sun warmed their heads, reminding Kate that she had forgotten to pack a hat. After a while they found a bench painted a bright blue that was partly shaded by tall trees and sat down.

"What a glorious day," said Amanda. She stared out at the lake and for a moment, all Kate could think of was those young women who spent their days watching the sea for their fishermen fathers, brothers, lovers to come back.

She shook off the disquieting feeling. "Yep, it's beautiful." She stared at the sparkling waters of the lake, wondering what was going on back at the station. "I should probably drop in on the Gimli detachment," she mused out loud.

Amanda turned to look at her. "Seriously?" she said. "Serious-ly?"

Nonplussed, Kate backed off. "As a courtesy," she offered. "I don't have to."

"Good," said Amanda, turning back to stare at the lake.

Geez. What the heck was that all about? Amanda had insisted on leaving the cell phone behind, and Kate figured she would have to find a pay phone somewhere to check in with McKell. And clear-ly she would have to do it without the girl catching on.

Fortunately, she had a plan.

"So," she said nonchalantly, stretching out her legs and cross-ing them at the ankles. She had worn a pair of blue pedal pushers, a white tee-shirt, and her walking sandals, where Amanda wore denim shorts and a cantaloupe-colored tank top that showed off her golden tan. "It's your birthday this week."

Amanda looked at her in surprise. "That's right." She started to smile then something flitted behind her eyes and she turned back to watching the lake. "It's no big deal."

Kate studied her niece. No big deal? Since when did a twenty-three-year-old think her birthday wasn't a big deal? In a family that made every birthday a royal affair with a special dinner, a homemade cake and a shower of gifts?

What the *hell* was going on with the girl?

"How about some ice cream?" asked Amanda suddenly. She stood up. "Come on, my treat." She turned her back on the lake and walked away, leaving Kate to trail thoughtfully behind her.

* * *

Mindful of her already demanding exercise regimen, Kate turned down Amanda's offer of an ice cream cone and suggested they go their separate ways and meet up at the car in an hour or so.

"I can come with you," said Amanda, turning away from the ice cream vendor parked near Centre Street. She licked her one-scoop maple walnut ice cream to keep it from dripping down the cone. "I'm not looking for anything particular."

Kate smiled. "But I am," she said cheerfully. "Now, make yourself scarce."

Amanda stared at her blankly before comprehension dawned. "Oh! Really, Aunt Kate, you don't have to—"

"Oh, for Pete's sake, Amanda!" Kate laughed. "Do you honestly think I'm going to let your birthday pass without a present? Go!"

Amanda hesitated a moment more, then grinned. With a wave of her free hand, she turned and leisurely strolled up the street, licking her ice cream, followed by every male gaze in the vicinity. Kate watched until she disappeared down a side street and turned to survey her options.

The street unfurled in front of her, filled with quaint shops and businesses featuring polar bears and dwarves on their front windows rubbing shoulders with steel and concrete buildings whose no-nonsense signs proclaimed them to be the ministry of this or that. Men and women in summer business attire—short-sleeved shirts and slacks or skirts—went in and out of the government buildings carrying briefcases or talking into their cell phones. They stood out in sharp contrast to the tourists who, like Kate and Amanda, wore shorts and pedal pushers in summer colors.

Kate blinked. She had no idea where to go. Finally she walked back to the ice cream vendor, an older man with a large gray mustache and a small white cap on his balding head.

"Excuse me, where would I find a pay phone?"

He paused in wiping down the small counter and looked past Kate. "Hmm. Used to be a lot more around, but now everyone's got a cell phone." He looked at Kate. "You can borrow mine if you like."

Kate smiled her appreciation. "Thanks, but it's long distance."

He shrugged. "Then your best bet is by the post office, on Fifth Avenue."

Kate got directions from him and set out. The breeze off the lake was cool, counteracting the warmth of the sun. It felt good to feel warmth on her skin again, after the long winter they had survived. According to the ice cream vendor, the post office was a few blocks up, parallel to the boardwalk. She kept her eyes open, just in case she saw a pay phone. The traffic on Centre Street was slow but steady, and she saw a lot of Ontario plates, plus a few Saskatchewan ones. She passed a side street and saw a small water park with kids playing and mothers keeping a watchful eye on them, with the occasional dad thrown in for leavening. Everyone wore shorts and sandals. Some of the young girls wore halter tops that didn't leave much to the imagination, but Kate told herself to stop being such an old prude. Still, what were their parents thinking?

Finally, she found the post office, but no pay phone. This was ridiculous. Sneaking around, looking for a way to contact her constables. She would just tell Amanda that she needed her cell phone. Period.

With a sigh, she looked around, trying to decide what to do next. Across the street was a store that took up the whole block. It had a two-storey façade and lots of display windows. The sign hanging over the doorway proclaimed:

PETTERSON'S

Est. 1897

She could see clothes in one of the windows. What the heck, maybe she would find something there for Amanda's birthday.

To her surprise, the store was high-end and contained an eclectic assortment of goods—everything from fishing rods to evening purses. She wandered around for half an hour, looking at clothes and paralyzed with indecision. What would Amanda like? She always wore tee-shirts and jeans or shorts, but surely a young woman had need of fancier clothes? But where would she wear them in Mendenhall? Of course, Mendenhall was only an hour away from Winnipeg. Maybe she should get the girl something she could wear on an evening out with Trepalli.

"Is there anything I can help you with, my dear?"

Kate turned to find a woman staring up at her. It wasn't often adults looked up at her, seeing as she was only five foot three, and the effect was a little disconcerting. The woman had to be at least seventy and was built round and sturdy, with green eyes sharp and clear, and white hair in an impeccable bun.

"Ma'am?" said Kate, more to give herself time to recover than because she hadn't understood. The woman wore a severely tailored dress with a round neckline and short sleeves, and with the wildest floral print Kate had ever seen. Unless she was in a jungle, this woman would not go unnoticed.

"You've been staring at the clothes here for quite a while," said the woman with a smile. Fuchsia lipstick. "Perhaps I can help."

Kate sighed. "I don't think so," she said glumly. "I can't think of what to get for my niece's birthday."

"How old is she?" asked the woman.

"Turning twenty-four."

The woman turned to glance around the clothing racks. "What kind of clothes does she like?"

"Jeans. Tee-shirts. Hoodies."

"Oh, dear." Despite her words, the woman's expression sharpened with interest. "A challenge." She took a few steps down the aisle, her gaze flitting from one rack to another. "What colors does she favor?"

For the next ten minutes, the woman proposed and Kate demurred, until they finally stood empty-handed by the sales counter. Two racks down, a saleslady was pulling out various sizes of capris from a sales rack.

"I'm sorry for wasting your time," said Kate. She decided she liked the older woman, who seemed determined to find something that would please Amanda.

"Nonsense," said the woman. "I like to keep my hand in, although it would seem I am losing my touch." She smiled to show she was joking.

"Are you the owner?" asked Kate.

"With my husband," said the woman. She stuck her hand out. "My name is Alice Petterson."

Kate shook her hand, mindful of maybe-arthritic bones. "Kate Williams. Nice to meet you. Family-owned, I take it?"

"For over a hundred years," said Alice Petterson proudly. "Our children run the store, now. Jakob and I help out once in a while." She eyed Kate shrewdly. "Where are you from, then?"

Because, of course, everyone in Gimli would know the Pettersons and their store.

"Just down the road a bit," said Kate. "Mendenhall."

"You'll be renting a cottage, then."

Kate almost laughed. The woman reminded her too much of herself. She would have made a good interrogator.

"We are indeed. On Fireweed Road, on Stony Point. Beautiful spot."

The woman's eyebrows rose. "Really?"

Kate hesitated. "Yes. Why? You don't think it's beautiful?"

"It is indeed a lovely spot," said Alice hastily. She slid a glance sideways at Kate and quickly looked away.

"All right," said Kate. "What?"

A tinge of pink colored Alice's cheeks and she laughed sheepishly. "It's nonsense. Just stories from years ago about the point being haunted."

Kate smiled but couldn't control the shiver that raced up her spine and spread over her scalp.

CHAPTER 3

AMANDA HAD picked up a whitefish at the pier, and that's what they had for dinner, with fresh greens and baby carrots in butter and ginger. For dessert, Amanda whipped some cream and served it on top of early strawberries.

Trust the girl to find the freshest food around.

"That was delicious," said Kate as she got up from the porch table. "No, sit. You made supper, I'll clean."

"How about some coffee?" asked Amanda, ignoring Kate and taking her dishes into the kitchen. "I even have decaf."

Kate consulted with her stomach and they both reached the same conclusion. "No, thanks," she said. "I don't think I can fit any more in. Now, shoo. I'll make coffee for *you*."

Amanda shrugged and disappeared into her room, only to re-appear a moment later with a book in hand. She went into the sun porch and sat in one of the wicker chairs, curling her feet under her. Kate watched her through the kitchen window as she placed ground coffee in the French press. The sun was low and sent long shadows into the porch. Amanda's book was in shadow, but Amanda wasn't reading anyway. Her gaze was far, far away. Her fair hair looked burnished in the reddish glow. Kate studied her niece for a moment, bothered by something she couldn't quite put her finger on.

She put the kettle on the burner and went to work stowing the dishes in the dishwasher and wiping down the counters and the table. When the water was hot enough, she poured it in, then found a mug featuring the iconic Gimli Viking and prepared her niece's coffee the way she liked it: a touch of cream and a smidgeon of honey.

"Here you go," she said, walking into the sun porch. She set the mug down on the wicker coffee table in front of Amanda.

"Thanks, Aunt Kate." Amanda set her book down and reached for the mug. "Going to come and sit?"

"In a minute," said Kate, and she went back inside before Amanda could ask any more questions.

She went to the refrigerator and felt around on top until she found her cell phone. She was embarrassed by the surge of relief she felt at holding it in her hands. Good grief. Was she addicted to the darned thing?

She headed out the front door, closing it silently behind her, and stood on the front stoop for a while, checking for missed calls and text messages. The sun edged past the corner of the cottage on its way to setting and chased the shadows away from the front stoop.

Two missed calls, from Rose and from Bert. Rose probably wanted to check up on her daughter. Kate calculated the time difference and decided it was still early in Montreal. No text messages. Rose hadn't quite caught on to texting. Kate realized she was feeling smug and grinned. Until a few months ago, she hadn't even known what texting was. Even now, it took her ten times as long to write out a message as it did Amanda. And it was exhausting.

First she'd call the station. Then she'd call Rose back. She'd save Bert for last.

She punched in the number for the Mendenhall Police Department and while it rang, she took the steps down to the walk and headed down the driveway, intent on scouting out a good route for her run in the morning. The trees sent long, questing shadows across the road and it occurred to her that she hadn't seen or heard another car in all the time she'd been here.

"Mendenhall Police," answered Constable Martins on the second ring.

"Evening, Constable," said Kate cheerfully. "Miss me yet?"

Martins laughed and she immediately relaxed. All was well with her station. Martins never laughed when he was stressed.

"Hi, Chief," he said. "How's cottage life?"

The question caught her by surprise and she stood looking at the trees across the road for a moment. How did she like cottage life? She studied the pine and ash trees, the wildflowers filling the ditch along the road, and the darkening sky.

"Haven't made up my mind," she said.

"Give it a chance," he advised. "It'll grow on you."

Sure. Like moss. "So, how are things in Mendenhall?"

"Oh, you know. Pretty quiet for now. It'll pick up in a few hours, as soon as the rowdies hit the bars."

With a shock, Kate realized that she'd lost track of the days. This was Saturday. She'd only been here one day. Less than twenty-four hours. And she had another seven days to go.

Dear Lord.

"Couple of fender benders. Some kids let the cows out of Stuart McNall's paddock and they got onto the highway." She could almost see him running his finger down the log book that she insisted they keep up, even though everything eventually got input into the computer log.

"Oh," he continued, "and a Mrs. Carmody reported that some-one stole clothes off her clothesline."

Kate could hear the smile in his voice. She finally started walk-ing again and turned right at the end of the driveway. She wanted to see where the road led.

"Kids?" she asked.

"Probably teenagers. The only things stolen were her teenage daughter's underwear."

"They still do that, eh?"

He laughed again. "I guess. It's kind of creepy, but I suspect hormones at work, not a nefarious plot."

Kate grinned at nothing. Was it wrong of her to miss the station? She wanted to ask if DC McKell had checked in, but that would be insulting to the deputy chief. He would have dropped by already, she was sure, and would probably check in again tonight. Her station was in good hands.

"All right, then," she said. "Call me if anything comes up. Not that I don't trust you to handle things, of course."

"Of course," he repeated, almost seriously.

Kate said goodbye and tucked the phone into her pocket. The temperature was starting to cool down and she debated going back inside for a sweater, but decided against it. She was only going down the road a bit. Maybe only as far as the neighbor's house.

And if the neighbor happened to be out, why, she might just introduce herself and strike up a conversation. That would be the neighborly thing to do.

She breathed deeply of the sweet air, trying to make out the different scents: that was sweet clover, definitely, and... was that wild roses? She glanced around but couldn't spot the delicate wild rose plant in the glare from the setting sun.

She strolled past the screen of pine trees that separated their cottage from the house next door and took her time, studying the two-storey house carefully. It looked just as dilapidated from the front as it did from the back. A covered porch ran the length of the front, and two dormer windows were set in the roofline. Although a rocking chair sat on the porch, no one was around. The front lawn needed a good trim.

So much for meeting the neighbor. Her thoughts floated back to Alice Petterson, at the store in Gimli. She had been embarrassed to share the rumor about the point being haunted, but she had still done it. In Kate's experience, people didn't share embarrassing stories without a reason.

The road petered out just past the neighbor's house. It became a trail that led through the mix of pine, maple, and poplar trees to the edge of the point. The underbrush was sparse, with only pine cones and fallen leaves from seasons past littering the ground. The trees were large and spaced far enough apart that she could see the silver glimmer of water at the end of the point.

A weathered picnic table waited at the top of the embankment, and a set of rickety steps led down to the rocky beach. From her vantage point, Kate could see the cottages across the small bay. Kids still played outside, but lights were starting to come on in the cottages.

A cool breath of wind found the back of her neck, and she shivered. Time to go. She turned and headed back down the path to the road. She pulled out her cell phone as she walked. She should call Rose before it got too late. She punched in Rose's number and walked out of the trees and onto the road while the phone rang at the other end three, then four times. Finally the answering machine came on, inviting her to leave a message.

Well, it was Saturday night, after all. Rose and John were probably out.

"Hi guys. It's me. Just returning your call. Amanda and I are in Gimli and we've already been canoeing. You'll be happy to know I didn't fall in. All is well here. I'll call you tomorrow." She broke the connection and was punching in Bert's number when something made her look up.

At first, she didn't see anything out of the ordinary, then a movement in the shadows on the road caught her eye. Amanda stood on the road on the other side of the neighbor's house, her arms wrapped around herself as if she were cold. They were still a little too far apart to speak without raising their voices, so Kate waved in greeting. Instead of waving back, Amanda just stood there.

Kate kept walking, trying not to hurry.

"Hi," she said when she was finally close enough.

"You left," said Amanda. Something in her tone made Kate look at her closely. Amanda's face was tight.

Kate smiled, trying to ease her niece's tension. "I was trying to figure out a route for my run tomorrow morning." She pointed over her shoulder at the end of the road. "We're the only houses on this point. There's a picnic table back there and a nice view."

Amanda nodded and turned back toward their cottage without a word, leaving Kate to follow.

Kate glanced down at where her niece had been standing. The spot was even with the trees that separated the two houses, as if Amanda had been reluctant to go past the property line.

CHAPTER 4

THE WEEPING came again that night. Kate blinked awake and rolled over to look at the time on her cell phone. One-fifteen, just like last night. She pushed the blankets away and reached for her sweatshirt lying at the foot of her bed, then slipped her feet into a pair of flip flops she had set on the floor next to her bed.

The house was quiet and cool. She made her way to her bedroom door and opened it, intending to go to the back yard and persuade the woman to talk to her. On impulse, she paused instead in front of Amanda's door and leaned closer to listen. After a moment, she heard a muffled sound and without thinking, she opened her niece's door.

"Amanda?" she spoke into the darkness. She could hear Amanda's ragged breathing and then her niece said something unintelligible. Kate reacted to the distress in her voice and hurried over to the bed. "Wake up, pumpkin." She shook Amanda's shoulder and jumped back in alarm when Amanda suddenly sat up and cried, "No!"

"Amanda," said Kate firmly. She didn't dare touch her niece again, for fear of throwing her into a panic. "Amanda, wake up."

Wasn't there a light on her bedside table? Kate leaned over and felt for it, while listening to Amanda's agitated breathing. Finally she touched something hard and closed her hand around the base of a lamp. After a bit of fumbling, she found the switch and turned the light on.

Amanda turned a wild-eyed face to her and Kate swallowed hard. Holy cow. What the hell had the girl been dreaming?

"Are you awake?" She sat cautiously on the edge of Amanda's bed and watched as awareness returned to her niece. She rubbed a hand up and down Amanda's bare arm, more to reassure herself than her niece. "Better?"

Amanda nodded and laughed shakily. "Wow. That may just have been the worst nightmare I've ever had."

Kate leaned in and hugged her awkwardly. "Want to tell me about it?"

Amanda shrugged. Already she was starting to relax as the nightmare receded. "I don't remember much. Something about drowning." She shivered and pulled up the blankets. "That is *so* not the way I want to die."

Kate's eyebrows rose. "You have a preference?"

Amanda grinned. With her hair all mussed up and loose around her face, she looked ten years old. She smelled of baby powder. "Well, sure, don't you? For instance, I wouldn't want to die in a fire, or of some horrible disease, or of hunger or exposure." She thought for a moment. "Ideally, I'd just fall asleep and never wake up."

Kate laughed. "I hope you get your wish, but only in another eighty years or so."

A yawn caught Amanda by surprise and she barely covered her mouth in time.

Kate patted her on the shoulder and stood up. "All right, I get the message. Think you can sleep?"

"Sure," said Amanda. "Why wouldn't I?"

Ah, youth. "All right. See you in the morning."

Kate closed the door behind her and debated going back to her own bed. Finally she headed for the kitchen and the sun porch, knowing there was no way she would be able to fall asleep again so soon. She glanced at the clock on the microwave. One-thirty. Too late to call Bert. He'd been out, too, when she called him back earlier. She'd have to wait until morning to talk to him.

She went to the sun porch and opened the outside door. The cool night air kissed her face with humidity and the scent of water. She went down the few steps to the flagstones and stood listening at the night. Nothing but frogs and crickets, and the sound of water lapping the shore. Her crying woman, if that's what she'd heard, seemed to be done for the night.

This was crazy. Tomorrow, she'd walk over to the house and knock on the door. If someone was in distress in that house, she wanted to know about it.

A light caught the corner of her eye and she looked up at the pine trees. She walked closer, her flip flops brushing the thick grass, trying to make out the light more clearly. Pushing the boughs aside, she caught sight of a soft light, almost like a lantern, floating up the side of the house, as if someone were climbing the stairs.

Only, there were no outside stairs, she suddenly remembered. No stairs and no balcony on that side of the house.

CHAPTER 5

I T MUST have been fireflies.

Kate sat on the couch in the sun porch, her feet up on the coffee table, staring at the sparkling waters of Lake Winnipeg through the cottonwoods at the bottom of the yard. It was going to be another beautiful day, she thought as she stirred her coffee. Too bad she felt like something the cat dragged in and didn't have the heart to eat. She had tossed and turned in bed for three hours before finally deciding it was late enough to get up and make coffee.

She realized she'd been stirring her coffee for a while and pulled the spoon out to rest on the low table in front of her.

There was no outside staircase leading to a second floor, and no balcony. She hadn't seen either one yesterday when she and Amanda paddled around the point. And she hadn't seen one when she walked past the house at sunset.

Therefore, the light she'd seen must have been a firefly. One that had a pattern of climbing high at one-fifteen in the morning.

"You're up early."

Kate jumped and sloshed hot coffee over her pyjama bottoms. With a hiss of pain, she set the mug down, stood up, and pulled the cloth away from her thigh.

"Sorry, Aunt Kate!" said Amanda. "I thought you heard me."

She pushed open the door from the kitchen and came into the porch. "Do you need a cloth?"

Kate shook her head. Already the sting was easing. "Just caught me by surprise," she said, sitting back down. She picked up her mug again and sipped, eyeing her niece over the rim. "How'd you sleep?"

"Fine," said Amanda airily. She flopped down next to Kate, threatening the stability of the cup, and Kate put it down again with a sigh. "Sorry about last night."

Kate examined her niece, noting that the dark circles seemed a little darker this morning. Despite Amanda's cheerful words, the usual sparkle was missing from her eyes and there was a tightness in her smile. Kate wished she could blame it all on the nightmare, but Amanda had been a little off for a couple of weeks now.

The kid was clearly working too hard. She'd forgotten how to relax.

"Want me to top up your coffee?" asked Amanda, suddenly getting up.

Kate silently handed her the mug and Amanda disappeared back into the kitchen. Maybe coming here hadn't been such a good idea. Neither one of them was sleeping well, what with that poor woman next door... But, as Amanda had pointed out, it wasn't easy to find a rental cottage in the area at this time of year, especially one so reasonably priced.

"We should go for a drive today," Kate called impulsively.

Amanda returned with two mugs and handed one to Kate. "Where do you want to go?"

"Let's go to Hecla Village," she said as Amanda settled in one of the wicker chairs. "It's a restored Icelandic village." Or so Bert, McKell, and even Charlotte, the department's only admin staff, had informed her.

"Sure," said Amanda.

"Good," said Kate, ignoring her niece's lack of enthusiasm. "It'll be fun."

After breakfast, they packed a couple of bottles of water—Kate had read that there was a guest house that served food—and set out in the Explorer.

It took just under an hour to reach the island. They avoided the highway, driving along the old road that followed the contours of the lake until they reached the bridge. Kate hadn't checked the weather forecast, but judging by the cloudless blue sky and sunlight glittering on the waves, it was going to be another beautiful day.

They found the village and joined a guided tour of the old schoolhouse, the boarding house, the church, the dock, the ice house, tool shed, general store... After a while, Kate realized she now knew way more about the Icelandic heritage of Manitoba than she had ever expected—or wanted—to know. At the general store, she caught Amanda's sidelong glance and motioned her to the back of the group. When they were a little behind the dozen or so tourists in the group, Kate leaned over to Amanda and whispered, "What do you say we make a break for it?"

Amanda grinned, and for a moment she was her old self. "Let's," she whispered back. They quickly made their way out of the dark wooden building into bright sunlight, and stood looking around at the restored village.

"I hear there are some nice hikes around here," said Amanda, looking up at the sky. Today she wore a pair of pedal pushers the shade of lime sherbet and a bright yellow tank top under an orange and green plaid, short-sleeved shirt that was open. Her hair was up in a ponytail and she had sunglasses perched on top of her head.

Kate glanced down at her own pedal pushers—white—and sandals and debated whether or not her clothes and feet would survive a hike. They finally settled on the short hike to the lighthouse. She figured the view alone would be worth the sand between her toes, but by the time they arrived at the lighthouse, Kate was rethinking the idea.

"My stomach thinks my throat's been cut," she complained as

they sat in the sand to watch the waves lap at the shore. She pulled her water bottle out of her fanny pack and took a long swig.

"Here you go," said Amanda and Kate looked around to find her niece handing her a granola bar.

Kate eyed the bar and the small daypack Amanda carried on her back. "I don't suppose you've got a cheeseburger in there?"

Amanda laughed. "There's a hotel on the way back. We passed it just before we got to the village." She pulled out her own water bottle.

Kate raised her knees and leaned her arms on them as she munched on the bar. This was lovely. And the hike had been nice, too. Her thoughts wandered back to Mendenhall and she found herself wondering how Saturday night had been, and if anyone had spent the night in the station's "guest" quarters. If she were back there, she would have run down to the station by now to check up on things, before running back. She hadn't run since Friday. If she didn't get a run in today, she was going to pay for it in sore muscles and a bad back.

"Aunt Kate?"

"Yes?" She glanced at her niece and found Amanda watching her cautiously, which perked her attention. "What is it?"

"Is there any way we can find out who lives next door?"

Well, well, well. Kate studied her niece's face and decided that Amanda's expression was a little too casual. She was sitting cross-legged in the sand, her sandals next to her and her water bottle in hand.

"I expect there is," said Kate. She swallowed some water and put the cap back on. "Why?"

Amanda took her time answering, as if she was trying to find the right words. Finally she looked at Kate. "I don't know about you, but that place is like an itch I can't scratch."

Kate hid a smile as she folded the granola bar wrapper and stuck it in her fanny pack with the water bottle. Voices floated out to them and they looked up to find an older couple coming around the bend of the trail. The woman nodded acknowledgement and Kate nodded back.

"Well, I *am* a little curious," she admitted. "But really, it's none of our business."

There was something in the girl's eyes, a cautiousness that gave Kate pause. Before she could do any more than note it, Amanda spoke.

"What about the crying?" she asked. "That's two nights in a row we've heard that woman crying. Shouldn't we do something about it?"

So Amanda *had* heard the crying last night. Once again, it had wound its way into her dreams. Or nightmares. Kate studied her niece's face, aware that Rose would disapprove of what Amanda was proposing. But Kate couldn't help but feel a rush of pride in the girl. And relief. For a few weeks now, it had felt as if Amanda was closing herself off from everyone and everything. It was good to see her take an interest in something outside her own thoughts.

"Well," she said thoughtfully, "it *is* public information."

"What is?" asked Amanda, confused.

"Ownership. We can check the tax rolls."

* * *

They had lunch at a fancy hotel on the island, which did not serve hamburgers and where the prices made Kate gulp, and were back at the cottage by mid-afternoon. Almost immediately, Amanda decided she wanted to make something special for dinner and drove off to Gimli with a wave. It was only after she left that Kate wondered if the grocery stores would be open on a Sunday.

She made herself a cup of coffee and went to the sun porch. She opened all the windows to let the breeze in, and immediately the sound of the water filled the small room, as did the scent of water, grass, and roses. With a sigh of contentment, she sat on the couch and pulled out her cell phone.

To her surprise, McKell answered the phone. "Mendenhall Police."

She used to bristle at his clipped tone but had grown used to it after a year and no longer allowed it to get to her. After all, he used it on everyone. Except maybe Charlotte.

"Hello, DC McKell," she said cheerfully. "How did you get stuck on the desk?"

"You know," said McKell conversationally, "we had a bet going about how long it would take you to call in. Trepalli came closest."

Kate laughed. "The pot calling the kettle black," she pointed out. Every time McKell left Mendenhall, whether for a conference or to check on his dying father, he phoned in at least once a day.

"Touché," said McKell, and she heard the smile in his voice. "We're a little short staffed with Friesen gone, so I'm relieving Martins for lunch."

Kate nodded. She'd forgotten that Friesen was on his way to Japan. Japan. It had never occurred to her to travel to Japan. Since it had been a quiet summer so far, she and McKell had decided not to pull anyone on shift. Trepalli, Friesen's usual partner, would work alone, or alternate with the other constables on his shift.

"Who's on?" she asked.

"Trepalli, Olinchuk, and Paterson," said McKell. "Olinchuk and Paterson are on patrol, and Trepalli is investigating a theft."

Kate's eyebrows rose. "A theft?" She leaned over and picked up her mug, then put her feet on the coffee table.

"Someone broke into a home while no one was there."

She tilted the phone away from her mouth and sipped. "What was taken?"

"Near as the homeowners can tell, just some clothes."

Kate frowned. "Clothes? I thought the clothes were taken from a clothesline."

"That was yesterday," said McKell. She could almost see him leaning back on the stool at the duty desk, his heels hooked on the cross bar, his free hand tapping a pen against the blotter. "Today's theft was inside a house a couple of blocks away."

Huh. Kate rested the hot mug on her belly and considered. "What clothes?"

"Underwear."

"Let me guess," said Kate grimly. "Teenage daughter?"

"Yep."

"Any connection between the two?"

"Only that they go to the same high school."

Well, that was hardly a connection. There was only one high school in Mendenhall.

"What about boy—"

"Chief?" said McKell gently.

She paused. "Yes?"

"I've got it."

Kate felt the heat crawl up her face and sighed. "Sorry, Rob."

"No worries," he said, and again she could hear the smile in his voice. "It's hard to let go."

Yes, he probably did understand how hard it was to let go.

Rob McKell had been in line to become Chief of Police when the old chief died, but Kate was hired instead. It had taken them a while to work it out, but they had. He was a fine police officer, despite the arrogance that peeked out at times.

"Right," she said. "So, aside from that?"

He was silent on the line and she checked to make sure she hadn't lost the connection. Finally he spoke again.

"Nothing serious. A small fire broke out in back of the hardware store on Main."

A picture of the store popped into Kate's mind. Brockman's Hardware was one of those old-fashioned hardware stores with crowded aisles and shelves stacked so high you needed a step stool to reach the top ones. Jim Brockman knew everything there was to know about hardware, and if he didn't sell it, it wasn't worth owning. While the front of the store faced Main Street, the back opened onto an alley and a small parking lot. She couldn't think of a single thing at the back of the store that might cause a fire.

"Arson?" she asked.

"Don't know yet." She could hear the shrug in his voice. "Fire Investigator just got here from Brandon."

Kate stared off into the distance, thinking about the alley. "Still," she said slowly, drawing the word out. "You have your suspicions."

McKell sighed. "Of course I have my suspicions," he said. "Brockman fired one of his employees yesterday, who by all reports, threatened Jim."

"You're bringing him in?" The minute she said it she wanted to recall the words. But McKell didn't react the way she had expected.

"As soon as the guy sobers up," he said quietly. "It'll be a while before we can question him."

"How much damage?" she asked, retreating to more neutral ground.

"The back of the store is charred, and they'll have to replace the door. Someone driving home from a party saw the fire and called it in."

"Lucky," said Kate.

"No kidding."

They hung up after McKell promised to call her if he needed her, and Kate sat drinking her coffee.

So, a fire, which was probably arson by a disgruntled ex-employee, and two thefts of girls' underwear. Panty raids were so sixties. Someone had probably dared someone else, and they'd eventually haul some young man in front of his parents to explain why he thought breaking into someone's house for panties was a good idea.

She sighed and just about dropped her cup when the cell phone rang right next to her. She pulled it up at eye level and saw Bert's picture appear. That was a nifty feature, one that Amanda had set up for her, since she had no idea how to do it. She pressed the icon and brought the phone up to her ear.

"Hi," she said.

"Hi, yourself," said Bert sternly. "Are you avoiding me, or are you having so much fun you haven't gotten around to calling me back?"

Kate laughed. "Are those my only choices?"

"Hmm," said Bert. "That's an interesting question. How are you enjoying the cottage?"

Kate glanced around at the sun porch with its wicker furniture and flowery cushions then looked through the window at the lake.

"It's lovely."

Bert laughed. She loved his laugh. It was full bellied and honest. He never laughed if he didn't think something was funny, and every time he laughed, she found herself smiling.

"You're bored out of your skull, aren't you?"

Kate blew a sigh out on a gust of air. "Good Lord—how do people do this?" she asked. "There's nothing to *do* here."

"The whole point of being at the cottage is to do nothing," said Bert. "You're supposed to wind down, chill out... whatever the current slang is."

"This isn't really my idea of relaxing," said Kate. She returned the mug to the coffee table and twisted herself until she was lying down on the sofa, her head on a cushion. "What's happening at your end?" Bert's job as deputy chief of Winnipeg Police Services was one of the things that had convinced her to give the relationship a try. He understood.

"Oh, the usual," he said.

Kate waited but he didn't add anything. "Like what?" she finally asked.

"Are you trying to get your fix through me?" asked Bert accusingly. "That's too sad for words. Stop thinking about work. Tell me what you've been up to."

So Kate told him about Gimli and Hecla Island, and about canoeing and finally about the crying woman.

"A woman crying in the middle of the night? Did you talk to her?"

Kate shook her head, even though he couldn't see her. "If there was anyone there, she didn't answer." She worked her sandals off and dropped them on the floor, and crossed one leg over the other. "Two nights in a row, though, and at the same time. It's a little weird."

"Huh. Tell me where the cottage is."

"It's a mile north of Gimli, right on the lake."

Bert was silent for so long that once again she checked her phone to see if the connection had been broken.

"Hello?" she finally said.

"Still here." His voice sounded funny. "Is there a big old house on a point of land anywhere near there?"

Now it was Kate's turn to be silent. Her foot stopped shaking as she absorbed his words.

"Yes," she finally answered. "Our cottage is on a point with another, older house. Why?"

"We used to go to Gimli every summer," said Bert, and she could hear the grin in his voice. "Me and my cousins. All the kids in the area thought that place was haunted."

A shiver ran up her arms despite the warmth of the sun porch, and she sat up, swinging her legs over the edge of the couch.

"Why did you think that?"

"We were kids. You've seen the place. Can you think of a better haunted house?"

Kate thought of the light she had seen climbing the non-existent stairs at the side of the house and shivered again. "Nope. It's pretty creepy. Who lives there?" She stood up and walked over to the window that faced the pine trees separating the two houses.

"No idea. We only ever saw it from the water as we cruised by."

"Amanda wants to check it out," said Kate. "Find out who owns it."

"Let me guess. She's bored, too."

Kate laughed and the creepiness fell away. "She needs to find a balance between boredom and working too hard. It's her birthday on Friday," she added quickly, before he could level the same accusation as McKell had. "Why don't you come out for dinner and stay the night?"

"I thought you'd never ask," said Bert with great satisfaction. "I'll bring wine."

"There's a nice bakery in town," said Kate. "I'll order a birthday cake."

"Just the three of us? Or is her beau coming, too?"

She hadn't thought of that. Maybe that was the reason Amanda was so mopey. She was missing Trepalli.

"I'll invite him," said Kate.

"Does he get to sleep over, too?" teased Bert. "Or are you going to make him sleep in a separate room?"

Good grief. Amanda was a grown woman and Kate wasn't her mother. If she wanted to sleep with the boy, that was her business. She had spent many nights at Trepalli's since she started dating him, but so far hadn't brought him home. Kate hoped she wouldn't have to have that talk with her niece. It was one thing for the chief of police's niece to be dating a constable. It was quite another for that constable to spend the night at the chief of police's house.

Just thinking about it gave her a headache.

CHAPTER 6

A T ONE-FIFTEEN, the soft crying woke her up and Kate lay in bed, staring at the dark ceiling and wondering how the woman next door managed it. Did she set the alarm to make sure she'd be up in time to cry? Did her husband come home every night at the same time and make her cry? Did she watch the late night movie every night and cry?

Kate was damned if she was going to rush out into the darkness for a third night in a row. The woman had ignored her every attempt to help. As long as no one was getting killed, Kate was willing to let the woman cry alone, if that's what she wanted.

Then a muffled scream reached her and she was out the door so fast she didn't have time to grab her sweatshirt. She rushed into the hallway, pushed open Amanda's door, and went over to the bed. She fumbled for the lamp's switch and turned it on, blinking in the sudden light. Amanda lay tangled in her bedsheets, her hands grasping at the covers, her eyes wide open and unseeing.

"Amanda." Kate sat on the edge of the bed and shook her niece's shoulder. "Amanda."

She thought she was ready, but when Amanda sat up suddenly, Kate jumped in surprise.

"Aunt Kate?" Amanda blinked in confusion, then awareness returned and she shuddered. "I was drowning. Someone was holding my head under."

Holy cow. Kate rubbed Amanda's arm comfortingly while wondering who was going to comfort *her*. "It was just a dream," she said firmly.

Amanda swallowed and looked at her. In the yellow glow of the lamp, her eyes looked huge and dark. "I never used to dream about dying."

Kate controlled a shiver and hugged the girl.

* * *

They woke late the next morning and were slow getting out of the cottage. It was almost eleven by the time they drove into Gimli and found the municipal office on Second Avenue. It was a lovely, two-storey building made of pale brick and stone that had a sign carved in the lintel that read: PUBLIC GIMLI SCHOOL 1915. Surrounded by lovely lawns and shrubbery, it was the least municipal-looking building Kate had ever seen. She had done her homework and had found the municipal lot number online. She'd had to ask Amanda how to do the search on her phone. She was ready when the clerk asked, and moments later the clerk called up the information on her computer.

"Sula Olafson," read the woman. She was short and round, with white hair that had to be premature given that she didn't look older than forty-five. Like many people around town, she had the blue Icelandic eyes of her Viking ancestors.

"Sula?" asked Kate uncertainly.

"A woman's name," explained the clerk. "Fairly common in these parts in my mother's day."

"How long has she owned the place?" asked Kate. Next to her, Amanda was busy scribbling down the name on a piece of scrap paper she had found in her purse.

"Well, she's been paying municipal taxes on it since 1959," said the clerk.

1959. Over fifty years. "Who owned it before that?" she asked impulsively.

The clerk looked over her shoulder at a young man sitting at the far end of the counter in front of a computer.

"John, can you check ownership of this property?"

John punched in the numbers as she reeled them off, and Kate couldn't help but marvel at the change technology had brought. Thirty years ago when she first starting policing, all this searching would have been done by hand in huge file rooms, and would have taken days, if not weeks.

"Arne Knutson," said John, looking up. "From 1932 to 1959. There are no records previous to that. That could mean that he built the house in 1932, or not. The town didn't keep records for the rural municipality back then."

Kate nodded her thanks and she and Amanda left the municipal building. They walked down the broad steps under a sky that threatened rain and stood in silence for a few moments.

The day was overcast and cool and both she and Amanda wore jeans and sweatshirts. Amanda had been very quiet all morning. Kate had suggested that she stay at the cottage but Amanda had shuddered in response and they had dropped the subject.

Kate was beginning to hate that cottage.

Finally, Amanda looked up.

"So, what's the next step?" she asked.

Kate shrugged. "Now we know her name. The next step is to introduce ourselves."

Amanda gave her a lopsided grin. "Mrs. Olafson doesn't strike me as very neighborly."

True. Still, that didn't mean they couldn't try. She remembered what she had been thinking last night just before Amanda had her nightmare.

"You know," she said slowly, "she might not live there alone."

Amanda looked down at her sneakered feet for a minute, thinking. Then she looked up.

"She lives alone," she said firmly.

A young couple emerged from the municipal office and came

down the steps, laughing. Kate glanced at them before turning back to Amanda.

"You seem pretty sure of yourself."

Amanda shrugged. "You only go that squirrely if you've been living alone for too long."

Kate grinned at her worldly-wise niece and put an arm around her shoulders. She turned Amanda toward the Explorer, which was parked a block away.

"Now, my dear, you need to make yourself scarce for, oh, say an hour." She glanced at her watch. Already well past noon. "Wait. How about lunch at that little deli we passed on the way here?"

"Sounds good," said Amanda. Her cheerfulness was a little too determined, but Kate let it go.

To Kate's delight, the deli specialized in perogies. They ordered the special—local sausages and homemade perogies—and Kate enjoyed every mouthful, even though she would need a nap afterward.

"That was good," she said at last, pushing away her empty plate. Amanda's lunch was barely touched and Kate frowned. "Not up to your standards?"

Amanda blinked in surprise. "What? Oh. I guess I'm just not as hungry as I thought."

Kate looked away. This damned vacation wasn't turning out at all the way it was supposed to. Instead of cheering Amanda up, it was having the opposite effect. She thought of suggesting they leave early, but knew her niece would immediately feel guilty. Five more days before they could go home. Oh joy.

The deli had a dozen small square tables and bright orange plastic chairs. A large picture window provided lots of daylight and a good view of the street beyond. It had started to rain and pedestrians ducked their heads and hurried their steps.

"I was thinking of inviting Bert to come up on Friday for your birthday dinner," said Kate, ignoring the fact that she'd already invited him. "What do you think?"

Amanda's smile, though brief, was genuine. "That would be lovely."

Bert and Amanda had taken an instant liking to each other. They'd met in the hospital, where Bert had come to make sure Kate was safe—she was—only to learn that Amanda, who had come to Mendenhall to check up on her uncommunicative aunt, had been shot. Amanda was the first to trumpet to the family that Kate had a "boyfriend," a description that still made her cringe. Boyfriends were for teenagers. She was fifty-four, for Pete's sake. And Bert was fifty-six. They were long past the girlfriend-boyfriend stage.

Of course, she wasn't really sure what they were. Companions? Sounded like something out of an English melodrama. Partners? She almost shuddered. No, definitely not.

"Aunt Kate?"

Kate looked up to find Amanda staring at her. "Yes?"

"What did you want to do now?"

Kate pushed the plastic chair back and stood up. The chair scraped along the floor, causing the young woman behind the meat counter to look up. Aside from Kate and Amanda, there were no other customers in the deli. Not surprising, since it was pushing two o'clock.

"Why don't you go shopping for your birthday dinner?" suggested Kate as she pulled her jacket from the back of the chair. She plucked a fifty dollar bill out of her jeans pocket and handed it to her niece, along with her car keys. "Something nice."

"Sure. What about wine?"

Kate raised an eyebrow. This must be what being a mother was like. Without a word, she pulled another thirty dollars out and handed the bills over.

Amanda grinned and stood up, too. She slipped on her thick fleece hoodie. "Where are you going?"

Kate smiled. "You'll find out on Friday. Let's go."

They walked back to the car in the intermittent rain and Amanda offered to drop Kate off wherever she was going, but Kate declined.

"Let's meet at the bakery on Fourth and Centre in about…" she glanced at her watch and did a rough estimate of how much time she'd need… "an hour and a half. Dessert will be on me." Everything was within easy walking distance and she had a jacket with a hood. She shouldn't get too wet.

"All right," said Amanda. "It won't take me that long, so I'll probably already be there."

Kate silently decided to go to the bakery first, to avoid any awkwardness. She watched Amanda drive away, haunted by the girl's eyes. What was going on with her?

She wished she had called Rose yesterday, but now she couldn't. Rose had some kind of antenna that twitched whenever Kate tried to keep anything from her. So now she couldn't talk to her sister without letting on how worried she was about Amanda.

She walked the two blocks to the Gimli Bakery. Not surprisingly, the bakery had more people in it than did the deli. What better time for a bit of sweetness than on a cold, rainy day?

There was a slip of a girl behind the counter and Kate guessed that this must be a summer job for her, since she was surely too young to be working for a living.

"How can I help you?" asked the girl. The name tag on her white cotton shirt read Heidi. Her pale brown hair had golden highlights and was up in a ponytail, and her blue eyes shone with youth and good health. Kate felt old just looking at her.

"I'd like to order a birthday cake," she said.

"Just a moment," said Heidi. She stepped through the open door behind the counter and murmured something to someone standing out of sight. An older woman emerged from the kitchen, wiping her hands on a striped dish cloth. She stood at least five foot ten and her hair was paler than the girl's but only because it had grey threading through it. Otherwise they had the same blue eyes, straight nose, and full mouth.

"You want a cake?" She motioned for Kate to follow her to the end of the counter, leaving the girl to deal with the customers who had accumulated behind Kate like tumbleweeds caught on a fence.

Ten minutes later, Kate had chosen Amanda's favorite cake—carrot—and told the baker what message she wanted on the cake. When she returned to the cash register to pay for the cake, it suddenly occurred to her to warn the young woman.

"Heidi," she said as she handed over the money, "I'll be meeting my niece here in about an hour. Can you pretend that we haven't already met?"

Heidi looked puzzled for a moment, then smiled. "The cake is for her?"

Kate nodded and the young woman promised she would help keep the secret.

It was still raining when Kate walked out. With a sigh, she pulled up her hood and adopted the huddled attitude of the other pedestrians as they negotiated the sidewalks with their oversized umbrellas.

Her jeans were damp along the thighs by the time she entered Petterson's. She stood at the entrance and tried to shake off most of the water before going inside.

She should have kept the car and made Amanda walk.

She wandered through the store, heading for the clothing section, and passed by a tiny perfume counter where she paused for a moment. But she couldn't remember Amanda ever wearing perfume, and she moved on.

The floors of the store had to be original hardwood. They were scuffed and worn, and creaked under foot. Kate decided she loved them.

There were a surprising number of people in the store, from young mothers or fathers with children in strollers to elderly women at the scarf counter trying to decide on a color.

"Couldn't stay away?"

Kate turned to face the older woman she had met yesterday. What was her name again? She almost panicked but then the name floated into her memory, a gift from the memory gods who were playing fickle with her lately. It helped that it was the same name as the store.

"Mrs. Petterson," she said with a smile. "When are the kids back?"

"Next week," said Mrs. Petterson. Today her white hair was up in a loose chignon that seemed to defy gravity, and Kate envied her the ability to look so effortlessly elegant. Her own hair always fought to escape any kind of confinement. Maybe it was time to consider cutting it short, and learn to live with looking like a billiard ball with hair.

"Have you found something for your niece?" asked the older woman. She wore a smart cream-colored pant suit with short sleeves and green buttons, with a silk scarf in a flamboyant flower print draped loosely around her neck.

A young girl with a name tag that read "Jennifer" came up to them and stopped at a respectful distance.

"Excuse me, Mrs. Petterson," she said.

"Yes, dear?"

"Do you know where Mr. Petterson is? One of the suppliers wants to talk to him."

"Try the storage area," said Mrs. Petterson and the girl left.

Mrs. Petterson turned back to Kate. "What are her interests?"

For a moment, Kate didn't know what she was talking about. She replayed their conversation and realized she meant Amanda.

"Well, she's a chef."

Mrs. Petterson's eyes lit up. "We have a wonderful kitchen section," she said. She placed her hand on Kate's elbow and started leading her. "I'm sure we'll find something for her there."

They went past the children's wear, the shoe department, the seasonal items department with its bright beach towels and patio furniture—the store was much larger than she had thought—and finally stopped in front of three rows of shelves that contained everything from blenders to knives behind a locked glass-fronted cupboard.

Kate stared at the bright yellows and blues of the egg beaters, the stainless steel bowls, the complicated-looking-not-to-mention-large implements that would take up most of her counter space. She had no idea what most of them were for.

Two women browsed different aisles, looking perfectly at home.

Kate looked at Mrs. Petterson. "Maybe I could get her a gift certificate?"

Mrs. Petterson patted her on the hand. "Nonsense. A girl should get a real gift on her birthday."

That was fine for Mrs. Petterson, but Kate had no idea what was good enough for a professional chef and what wasn't. Considering the way Amanda looked lately, Kate couldn't think of any gift that might cheer her up. Except maybe Marco Trepalli.

Hmm. She had forgotten to invite the boy. She should do that soon. His presence would surely take the heat off Kate's sure-to-be-pathetic birthday gift.

Cheered, she strolled through the aisles with Mrs. Petterson, discussing the kind of catering Amanda did.

"One thing a caterer never has enough of are serving platters," said Mrs. Petterson. She pointed to a rack with colorful platters. "They get broken or are never returned. For the big jobs, they use those thin metal platters, but some jobs call for real dishes."

That was a good idea. Amanda had only been in business for a few months and she was still using disposable dishes for many of her jobs. Kate pulled one of the platters out, trying to decide if its colorfulness would make up for its fragility.

"How are you enjoying your cottage?" asked Mrs. Petterson.

Kate had conducted enough interrogations in her time to recognize a soft lob when she heard one.

"It's lovely," she said. "But to be honest, I may not be the cottage type."

Mrs. Petterson grinned, her green eyes mischievous. "I would never have guessed." She flicked a glance over her shoulder, as if checking to see if they could be overheard, and Kate resisted an urge to do the same.

"Have you met your neighbor yet?"

Ah.

"Not yet." She could feel her smile straining and tried to relax. It was natural curiosity, no doubt about it, and Kate was as guilty as the next person of being nosy, but the question immediately put the woman's friendliness under a different light. Still, this was an opportunity to do some digging of her own.

"How long has Mrs. Olafson lived there?" she asked, her hand lingering over turquoise linen napkins.

Mrs. Petterson's eyes widened in surprise at hearing the name but she quickly regained her composure.

"Sula and I were in school together," she said. "She grew up in that house. Her mother grew up in the little shack that was there before the house. If I had to guess, I'd say there's been an Olafson on the point for close to a hundred years."

And the house had been built in 1932. The dilapidation had to be fairly recent or the house would have fallen apart before now.

"It's a darned shame what's happened to the house," continued Mrs. Petterson, as if reading Kate's mind. "She tries to keep it up, but her heart isn't in it, not since her children ran away."

Kate stopped fingering linens and gave the woman her full attention. "Children?"

The woman nodded sagely and waited until a browser walked by before continuing.

"Sula and Malcolm adopted a girl way back in…" she paused to think for a moment. "1966." She smiled sadly. "A beautiful child. Sarah." She sighed.

Kate remained silent, willing Mrs. Petterson to go on. After a moment, she did.

"They'd only had her a few months when Sula got pregnant." She looked up at Kate and shook her head. "Isn't that always the way?"

Kate judged that she didn't really expect an answer.

"She gave birth to a boy."

Kate waited but Mrs. Petterson seemed to have succumbed to sadness. Her smiling mouth turned down at the corners and her eyes grew dull with memory.

"What was his name?" prompted Kate.

"Daniel. At first, he seemed like a perfectly normal little boy."

Hoo boy. This woman had the storyteller's gift of always leaving her audience wanting more. In this case, Kate wanted to shake the words out of her.

"Alice," said a man's voice behind Kate. They both turned guiltily to see a tall, thin, older man, perfectly bald, watching Mrs. Petterson reprovingly.

A tinge of pink crept up Mrs. Petterson's powdered cheeks. She turned to Kate.

"Allow me to introduce my husband, Jakob," she said. "Jakob, this is Kate Williams. She's staying at the cottage on Stony Point, next to Sula's."

Jakob Petterson looked sharply at his wife, as if suddenly understanding something. But he turned to Kate and shook her hand, saying only, "Very nice to meet you, Mrs. Williams. The point is a lovely spot."

"It is," agreed Kate. The man had the handshake of a bigger man and she tried not to wince as she rescued her hand from his grip. "Your wife was telling me a little bit about the history of the point."

His raised eyebrow told her he wasn't fooled, but there was a twinkle in his sharp blue eyes.

"Your cottage is relatively new," he said. "It was built in the '90s. Before then, the Olafsons owned the entire point. On the weekends, we would all motorboat up the lake to the point. We would picnic, swim, and later on, water ski." His eyes lost some of their sharpness as he remembered. "The Olafsons, Sula's parents, would feed us all, provide bunks for us, and send us on our way on Sunday afternoons."

Mrs. Petterson smiled up at her husband, and for just a moment, Kate could see the teens they had been, Alice with her long blond hair looking up adoringly at Jakob, who had cut a rakish figure in his white shirt and linen pants.

Well. Memory Lane was very nice, but she wanted to know about the current resident of the Olafson house. At the same time, she didn't want to spook the old man, who clearly disapproved of gossip. Kate had no problem with gossip. As long as it wasn't malicious, it served a real purpose in sharing information about friends and neighbors. And in policing.

"How many children were there in the family?" she asked.

"Six," replied Alice Petterson. She had tucked her hand in the crook of her husband's arm, as if that was where it belonged. "But Sula is the only one left."

Careful now, thought Kate. She desperately wanted to know more about Sula Olafson's children, sensing that this was where the heart of the story was, but knew better than to broach the subject around Alice Petterson's husband.

"When did she sell off part of the point?" she asked instead.

Alice and Jakob glanced at each other. Finally Alice shrugged and looked back at Kate. "It must have been about thirty years ago. After her husband died."

If Sula Olafson was a contemporary of Alice and Jakob, she was probably in her mid-seventies. That meant that her husband would have died when she was about forty. No children, no husband, no family left... No wonder the woman was a recluse.

"She lives there all by herself?" she asked, just to be sure.

"Yes," Jakob nodded sharply. "She prefers it that way."

Kate blinked. His statement did not invite further questions, but honestly, did he think she could just leave it there?

"Mr. Petterson?"

They all turned to see the same young girl who had asked Alice Petterson where her husband was.

"Yes, Jennifer?" said Jakob.

"There's a supplier here to meet with you, sir."

"Ah." Jakob turned to Kate. "I'm afraid we'll have to leave you to your shopping." Placing a hand over his wife's, which still rested on his arm, he began to lead her away.

Alice glanced back over her shoulder at Kate and shrugged apologetically. "Good luck," she said.

CHAPTER 7

I N THE END, Kate settled on three white porcelain platters—
one square, one oval and one rectangular—with a small
muted flower pattern in blues and yellows along the edges.
She added six yellow napkins and six blue napkins and got the
clerk at the store's service desk to wrap everything up in a box for
her.

The blasted thing was heavy and she was breathing a little
harder when she spotted the Explorer parked a block away from
the bakery. She tried the handles. Locked. Now she would have to
haul the gift into the bakery. Oh, well. It wasn't as if she was planning to surprise the girl.

Amanda was sitting facing the door and her eyebrows rose
when she saw the bag Kate was carrying. She opened her mouth to
speak but Kate lifted a warning finger.

"Not even a hint," she said.

There were only two other customers at the small round tables.
It was past the coffee break rush. True to her word, Heidi acted as
if she had never seen Kate before and soon Kate and Amanda sat
facing each other with coffee and strudel in front of them on the
mosaic table top.

As Kate demolished the pastry, she told Amanda what she had
learned about the house next door. She watched Amanda's expres-

sion go from still to curious and wondered again what was causing her normally vivacious niece to be so quiet. Her pastry remained mostly untouched.

"What was wrong with the boy?" asked Amanda when Kate finished.

"I don't know." Kate sipped her decaf coffee and stared out the window at the wet street. "Mrs. Petterson's husband showed up before she could tell me."

"Well, darn."

Yes, indeed. "You know," said Kate warningly, "it really is none of our business."

Amanda looked up quickly and blushed. "I know," she said. "But don't you want to help Mrs. Olafson? I mean, why does she cry every night?"

Every night at one-fifteen. A shiver coursed down Kate's spine and she shook herself.

"I think we should go over there and bring her a treat," continued Amanda.

Kate stared at her, suddenly confused. "A treat?"

"Yes, you know... A cake, or cookies. A way to introduce ourselves. She'll invite us in and we'll be able to assess if she needs our help or not."

Kate sat back and studied her niece. Amanda's cheeks were flushed and her blue eyes shone with enthusiasm.

"I think that's a great idea," said Kate cautiously. She wasn't at all sure it *was* a good idea, but didn't want to rain on Amanda's parade. "Do we have everything we need?"

Amanda pulled her purse forward from where it hung on the back of the chair and rummaged through it, eventually emerging with a pen. She pulled her unused paper napkin toward her.

"Let's see," she said as she began to write. "We could make a nice lemon loaf, or maybe chocolate chip cookies..."

* * *

Of course, by the time they returned home and made dinner, it was too late to do more than bake the cookies and set them to cool on the counter. The clouds had finally cleared and after the dishes, while Amanda was still spooning dough onto the cookie sheets, Kate wandered outside with her tea. She walked over the wet lawn to the stairs leading down to the dock, but didn't go down.

The cottage faced east so she couldn't watch the sun set, but the light of the setting sun burnished the surface of Lake Winnipeg and the waters disappeared into the mists of distance. The wind had died down and all she could hear was the lapping of the waves as they kissed the shoreline.

She sipped her peppermint tea and watched a couple of ducks fly over her head, their shapes silhouetted against the darkening sky, heading for the far shore. Or maybe they were geese.

"Want one?"

Kate jumped, sloshing a bit of tea over the rim of her mug. Amanda smiled innocently and held out a small plate with chocolate chip cookies stacked prettily.

Another sweet. When was the last time she had run? She had planned to run on Sunday, but they'd gone for a hike instead. A stroll, really. And she certainly hadn't done any kind of exercise today.

"You're looking at them as if they're poisoned," said Amanda, and there was no disguising the laughter in her voice.

"Not poisoned," said Kate glumly. She took one of the cookies. It was still warm. "I was just thinking that it was time I went for a run."

"Not tonight?" asked Amanda in sudden alarm. Kate glanced at her, then looked at the sky. It was definitely getting darker.

"Tomorrow," she said firmly. "It's getting too dark." The chocolate chips were melting all over her fingers and she took a bite. Soft, chewy, sweet. She closed her eyes, the better to savor the blissful morsel. "Wonderful," she said around a mouthful.

"I'll leave these with you," said Amanda, pushing the plate toward Kate. "I have to go back. The next batch should be almost ready."

"No, you don't," said Kate. She popped the rest of the cookie in her mouth and pushed the plate back toward her niece. "Take those back inside before I take another one."

Amanda laughed and headed back toward the cottage. Her slim build made her look taller. Of course, just about everybody was taller than Kate. She had learned to accept being five foot three inches tall, even though she'd always felt her size was a detriment to her career. Bert said she was five foot three going on six feet.

Tomorrow was Tuesday. Holy cow. Another four days before she could get back to her real life in Mendenhall.

Shaking her head, she impulsively descended the steps to the beach and crouched to wash her chocolate-smeared hand, which she then wiped on her jeans. It was cooler on the beach, since there wasn't a screen of trees to protect her from the slight breeze that had kicked up in the last few minutes. She took another sip of tea and jumped again when her cell phone rang, breaking the stillness. She quickly fished it out of her pant pocket and glanced at the screen. Rose.

"Hey, sis," she answered cheerfully.

"Hey, yourself," came Rose's voice. She sounded like she was next door, rather than on the south shore of Montreal. "How's the vacation going?"

"Great!" said Kate enthusiastically. She wandered down the beach toward the Olafson place, watching where she placed her feet. "This is a lovely place and the view is incredible."

There was a silence at the other end that lasted a few seconds before Rose came back with, "You're bored silly, aren't you?"

"Oh my God!" said Kate. "This week will never end!"

Rose giggled and Kate started laughing, too.

"How's Amanda?"

Kate shrugged. "She's baking chocolate chip cookies."

"Really?" said Rose. Kate could imagine her sitting in the sun room of her St. Lambert home, even though it would be dark there by now. The sun room was Rose's favorite place. "Is everything all right? Chocolate chip cookies are her comfort food."

Kate's eyebrows rose. "She's baking them for our neighbor. Maybe she figures they will comfort her, too."

She reached the trees separating her cottage from the Olafson land and paused. The boulder sat invitingly on the beach, a natural seat dividing the two beach fronts.

"Hang on," she said. She tossed the last of the tea out before climbing up the boulder to sit facing the water. She brought the phone back to her ear. "Okay, I'm back."

"Where are you?"

"Sitting on a boulder, looking over Lake Winnipeg. The sun has just about set and the water is quiet."

"Can you see the sunset?"

"Nope. But the lake is reflecting the last of the sunset colors. It's really pretty."

Rose sighed. "I wish I was there with you."

"I wish you were here, too," said Kate. She meant it. She'd last seen Rose and John two months ago, when she'd gone down with Amanda for a visit. Amanda had closed down her apartment and packed all her belongings—most of which had to be shipped. Kate's Mom, who lived in the same town as Rose and John, had been in fine form and had made her tourtieres, much to Kate's delight.

"How's Mom?"

"She has a beau, would you believe?" Rose's voice was filled with delight. "He's a former colonel in the army, a widower. She met him in church."

"Good for her!" said Kate. At seventy-eight, Mom was still very active in her community. She walked everywhere and seemed to be the social nexus for a group of a dozen or so seniors in her neighborhood. "Have you inquired about his intentions?"

Rose laughed. "I have, and Mom informed me that I was being nosy."

Kate grinned. "That's what children do," she said.

They chatted for a few more minutes before ringing off. Kate sat quietly for a while, absorbing the stillness of the lake. Somewhere in the distance, a loon called out. She rested her arms on her raised knees, aware that despite the padding in her bum, the boulder was growing uncomfortable. Finally, she punched in the number at the station and brought the phone up to her ear.

"Mendenhall Police," said Nick Martins.

"Hello, Martins," said Kate. "How's everything?"

"Chief," said Martins in acknowledgment. She could imagine him at the duty desk, perched on the high stool, the phone pressed between his ear and his shoulder. He had crinkly auburn hair just starting to recede and freckles all over his face. She always suppressed a smile when she saw him.

Her smile faded as the silence dragged on.

"Martins?"

"Yes, ma'am," he said at once. "We had a fire."

She relaxed. She already knew this. "Yes, at Brockman's Hardware."

"That was yesterday," said Martins cautiously.

Kate blinked, trying to parse out what he was saying. "Is there another fire, Constable?" she asked, her tone sharper than she had intended.

"Yes, ma'am," said Martins. "Over lunch, at the Wheatland Café."

Holy cow. She'd been in there often to pick up sandwiches or soup. "How did it happen? Any injuries? What's the damage?"

Martins answered her most important question first. "No injuries. Everyone got out as soon as the fire broke out. Firefighters were on scene right away and put it out. The kitchen's gone but the front part is intact. Of course there's smoke and water damage." He sighed. The Café was a favorite among the constables. "Nobody knows how it started yet. The DC is still there, along with Fire Chief Avramson and the fire marshal from Brandon."

Two fires in two days. In summer. In winter, there were always more building fires than in summer, principally chimney fires. In summer, the fire risk was to forests and crops more than to physical properties. It was highly unusual to have two fires in two days. Unlikely, even.

"Chief?"

"Yes, I'm still here. Have the DC call me when he gets back. Now, anything else? What about our panty raider?"

"He seems to have moved on," said Martins. "No new reports in Mendenhall, but I just received a report from Sidney that someone broke into a home overnight and ran off when the teenage girl woke up and saw him in her room. He'd stolen some of her underwear."

Kate suddenly noticed that the boulder felt cold on her bottom. She straightened her legs and worked her way down until she was standing on the beach.

"This fellow is escalating," she said grimly. It no longer sounded like something a teenager would do on a dare. "You should send out a warning to communities up the highway and tell them to watch for him."

"Already done," said Martins, and she thought she detected a note of reproof in his voice.

"Of course," said Kate apologetically. Of course. McKell would have ordered it the moment he realized. "Well, you know how to reach me if you need me. Don't forget to get the DC to call me."

"Yep," said Martins before ringing off.

Kate leaned back against the boulder, her gaze lost in the gathering darkness. She should have told Martins to call Brandon and Virden, and the other communities west of Mendenhall, to see if they had any reports of a panty bandit. She didn't like that he was now breaking into people's homes while they were inside.

In her experience, this kind of escalation never ended well.

CHAPTER 8

KATE TRIED to convince Amanda to go to bed, but once the girl realized Kate planned to stay up, her mouth thinned in determination and she put the kettle on.

"There's no point to both of us staying up," said Kate in a last-ditch effort.

Amanda concentrated on measuring out the coffee grounds into the glass carafe and didn't turn around. "Aunt Kate, have you ever dreamed you were dying?"

Kate shut up.

At night the overhead light in the kitchen cast a soft glow over the table and the tile floor. Romantic, maybe, but not practical to see what you were doing. Kate stepped down into the sun porch and found her reflection staring back at her. The wind sighed against the house and she could see an impression of movement in the darkness that was the yard. She knew it was the trees moving in the wind, but it still made her uneasy. It left her feeling exposed. A moment later, Amanda joined her, carrying a tray with cups and the French press.

There was no television in the house, not even a radio, so they played cards—a weird variant of Bridge that Kate and Rose used to play when they were growing up. Kate kept glancing at her watch but time moved excruciatingly slowly. McKell called but had nothing more to report.

After a while, Kate and Amanda gave up on the cards and sat talking desultorily about Amanda's catering business. It was only ten-thirty, and already Kate's eyelids had turned into sandpaper. Too many nights in a row of broken sleep.

"The only place in town with a commercial kitchen is St. Alban's Church," said Amanda. She poured herself more coffee and topped off Kate's cup. "I suppose I could rent it, but I'd have to vacate for their regular groups and on Sundays, when they have their communal kitchen. Besides, who wants to work in a basement?"

"You know you can use my kitchen for as long as you like." Even as she said it, Kate knew that Amanda's business was outgrowing the kitchen. More often than not, Kate would come home to find every surface in the kitchen occupied by bowls, mixers, and chopping boards. Amanda needed a bigger kitchen than Kate's.

Besides, Kate's stove was electric and Amanda wanted gas. Unfortunately, the only reason Amanda was making money was because she had no overhead costs. The minute she started renting, her profit margin would disappear.

"I know, Aunt Kate," said Amanda with a smile. "But I need more space. A bigger stove—even two. A big refrigerator. More counter space." She sighed. "If I'm going to stay in Mendenhall, I'll have to set up my own kitchen."

Kate's heart squeezed. That almost sounded like Amanda was planning to move out, maybe even out of Mendenhall. The wind picked up, flinging leaves against the windows.

"Are you thinking of leaving?" she asked softly. That darned kid had entered her life last February and weaseled her way more deeply into her heart, and now she was thinking of leaving?

Amanda shrugged. "I don't know. So far, Mendenhall is keeping me busy. I'm not ready to think about leaving. I like it there." A shadow crossed her face and she looked away from Kate.

"Pumpkin, what's the matter?" Kate asked gently. "You've been acting funny."

Amanda shrugged but couldn't help a smile at her childhood name. "I'm just tired," she said. "I thought this week would be more restful."

No kidding. Kate slumped back in her chair, studying her niece's profile. This week hadn't been restful at all.

"We could leave," she suggested. "No law says we have to stay."

"No, no," said Amanda quickly. "I'm sure things will get better."

Kate was no expert, but she was pretty sure that wasn't the right attitude for a holiday. Clearly, Amanda wasn't having any fun here, but she didn't want to go back home. Why?

"So what are you making for your birthday dinner?" she asked, trying to change the gloomy mood that had descended upon them. She glanced at the clock. Eleven-thirty. Dear Lord, would this evening never *end*?

Amanda looked up and grinned. "I was thinking steak and salad, with fresh berries and whipped cream for dessert. Nothing fancy."

Kate's eyebrow rose. Her idea of nothing fancy was oatmeal.

She pulled a magazine from the stack on the round glass-topped table and settled down to read. Amanda got up and fetched the book she was reading. She curled up on the couch and began reading, too. Soon enough, her eyelids drifted closed and her chin nodded to her chest.

Kate smiled. Years of shift work had inured her to her diurnal rhythm. She could sleep anywhere, anytime. Conversely, she could stay up when she needed to. She didn't like it, but she could do it.

At one o'clock, she set the magazine down and carefully made her way to the kitchen. It would be much shorter to use the sun porch door to reach the back yard, but the cooler air entering might wake Amanda.

Moments later, she stood outside on the front porch, looking up at the night sky, shivering in the cool breeze. With only the half-moon staring back at her, empty of warmth, and no nearby lights to blind her to the sky, the Milky Way spread before her in pale glory. Finally she pulled herself away and went down the steps. As she passed the sun porch, she glanced inside. Amanda was still fast asleep.

She crossed the lawn to the staircase and carefully descended to the beach. Once her sneaker touched the sand, she breathed a sigh of relief. She glanced up at the embankment but could only see the cottonwoods and bushes that hid the lawn.

The lake spread to her right like an ocean. Little waves lapped at the shore, whispering on the sand as they receded. Moonlight glimmered on the crests and provided enough light for her to make out the large boulder she had sat on earlier that day.

Worried that she had lost track of time, she hurried past the boulder and onto the beach below the Olafson house. Beyond the point, the cottages lining the shore across the tiny bay were dark and silent.

Unlike their own cottage, the Olafson house had no dock and no stairs leading down to the beach. There must have been a stair-case at one point. The Pettersons had spoken of descending on the house when they were teenagers and motor boating. But if there had been one fifty years ago, it was long gone.

She stared up at the ten-foot shelf and sighed. She was too old to be scrambling up mini-cliffs in the middle of the night. Espe-cially on someone else's property.

But she wasn't putting up with one more night of that weird crying without at least trying to find out who was doing it.

Fortunately, the shelf had been shored up against storm surges by rocks and it was relatively easy to climb up. Bushes and tough grasses grew at the top of the shelf, and as she hauled herself up, she thought of all the voles and mice that probably lived there.

Not a comforting thought.

The crying, when it came, was so soft that at first she thought it was the wind through the grasses. When she finally realized what it was, she hauled herself up the last few feet and cautiously poked her head above the shelf. All she could see was grass. Balancing on a too-small rock, she parted the grass and peered through to the house.

Her eyes had grown accustomed to the darkness and the moon cast enough light for her to make out the unkempt yard of the Olafson house. The breeze threaded through the long grass and weeds, like fingers ruffling hair. Moonlight reflected from the two doors at the back and the upstairs windows. There was no one on the porch or on the upstairs balcony.

Her gaze swept the yard as she tried to catch a movement, any movement, but she saw nothing. And yet, the soft crying persisted. She turned her head, trying to locate the woman from the sound, but the wind played tricks with her, first sending the sound to the north, where the summer kitchen was, then closer to the water, as if the woman were standing just over Kate.

In frustration, she hauled herself all the way up and over the edge, and rose stiffly to her feet.

"Hello?" she called softly. The crying immediately stopped and all she could hear were the crickets. She stood still while scanning the back yard from end to end. Where was the woman? The shadows by the pines that separated the Olafson property from her rental cottage were deep and Kate peered into them, trying to make out a shape.

"Are you all right?" she said softly. "I heard you crying..."

Nothing. The pine smell of the trees washed over her and she edged closer, trying to see. "Please let me help."

But the closer she got to the trees, the clearer it became that there was no one there. Where the hell was she? There was no way anyone could have slipped past her, and even if the woman had been on the porch or the balcony, she would have seen her entering the house.

The breeze lifted her hair on the back of her neck and she shuddered reflexively. She should have dressed more warmly.

Just to be sure, she walked the length of the trees, even going so far as to poke into the denser shadows. She caught a glimpse of light from the cottage on the other side of the trees, but otherwise the screen was thick and not easily penetrated.

She raised her head and turned toward the beach even before her brain registered the soft noise. She held her breath, waiting for it to repeat. She hadn't realized how the wind had risen until she tried to hear above its sighing, but finally she heard it again.

Sobbing. Someone was on the beach, sobbing.

She went from standing still to running in a split second, even as her brain tried to convince her that it was her imagination, that no one had gotten past her. She reached the wild grasses and sat down abruptly so she wouldn't kill herself falling down ten feet. Her sneakers found the retaining stones and she levered herself up and took the slope at a run. The sand slowed her down at the bottom, but a moment later she rounded the big boulder separating the Olafson beach from hers.

She finally stopped as the moon revealed what her brain had been telling her. There was no one on the beach. She glanced up but there was no one on the steps leading to the back yard of the rental cottage.

Then she heard the sobbing again and her head slowly turned toward the water.

Amanda. Amanda was wading steadily through the increasingly deep, cold waters of Lake Winnipeg, her arms out by her sides.

Without a word, Kate broke into a run.

CHAPTER 9

W E'RE LEAVING."

Amanda looked up from her hot chocolate.

"Honestly, Aunt Kate, I'm fine."

"You are not fine," said Kate grimly. "And we're leaving."

"Aunt Kate," said Amanda patiently, "I was sleepwalking, not suicidal."

They were sitting at the kitchen table. It was almost ten o'clock in the morning. The sun streamed into the sun porch and through the window above the sink, filling the kitchen with warm and golden light. Kate wasn't fooled.

By the time she had reached Amanda, the girl was already waist-deep in the water, and the action of the waves threatened to pull her under at any moment. She woke up the moment Kate touched her and Kate had to shake her out of her panic at suddenly finding herself in the cold waters of Lake Winnipeg. Kate dragged her out and hustled her into a hot shower, then she tucked her niece in bed. Amanda had fallen asleep before her head hit the pillow.

Kate, on the other hand, had stayed up all night, in a chair she had dragged in front of Amanda's door. No way was she calling Rose to tell her Amanda had drowned.

Now Kate stared at her niece resentfully. Except for faint circles under her eyes, Amanda looked none the worse for wear. Kate had no illusions about how *she* looked.

"When did you start sleepwalking?" she demanded. She knew she sounded accusing, but the girl had scared her. She never wanted to feel like that again. It was almost worse than when Amanda was shot. If she hadn't spotted Amanda when she did... They might never have found her body, let alone figured out what had happened to her. She shivered at the thought.

They were *so* leaving.

"Mom says I used to sleepwalk when I was a little kid," said Amanda. She blew on the hot chocolate and took a sip. True to form, she had heated up milk and melted grated Belgian chocolate into it, where Kate would have pulled out the cocoa. Kate hadn't even known they had Belgian chocolate in the cottage. Right now, she would settle for scotch.

"But she usually found me in the kitchen, pulling everything out of the cupboards."

Of course. Kate rotated her shoulders in an effort to work out the kinks. She hadn't pulled an all-nighter in years.

"She never told me about your sleepwalking," said Kate before taking a sip of her own hot chocolate. She had to admit that Amanda's was magnitudes better than her own cocoa and hot water would have been. "In any case, I've had about as much of this 'holiday' as I can stand."

Amanda sighed. "All right. But can we at least drop off the cookies to Mrs. Olafson?"

Kate shrugged. "Sure. Why not." As long as they were leaving.

* * *

The trees and flowers bordering the narrow road seemed to glow with health. The rain had washed the dust off all the pine and ash trees and bushes, and refreshed the colors of the wild roses, buttercups and flowers that looked like marigolds, only white. The air smelled fresh and clean and the day promised to be warm, even though right now it was a little cool. Kate was glad she had decided to wear a sweatshirt over her tee-shirt.

The Olafson house had a deep front porch that was in shadow as they walked up to it. Kate realized that their steps had slowed as they approached and she made a conscious effort to lengthen her stride.

The damned place spooked her. Especially after last night. She had heard someone crying, a woman. *Before* she heard Amanda. But there'd been nobody there. The only thing she could figure out was that the crying had come from an upstairs window, perhaps the one facing the screen of trees. Mrs. Olafson must have heard her call out and stopped crying. Some trick of acoustics had made the crying sound as if it were at ground level.

She glanced at Amanda. Her niece wore white pedal pushers and sandals, and a pale yellow cotton sweater with the sleeves pushed up. She carried a pretty tin filled with chocolate chip cookies. Kate had no idea where the tin had come from. Amanda had caught her hair up in a low chignon, a hair style Kate had never seen on her before. It looked old-fashioned but suited her.

"Ready?" Kate asked as they reached the stairs.

Amanda nodded and together they mounted the steps. Despite its dilapidated appearance, the porch was sturdy. A couple of coats of paint and it would be inviting and fresh. The house had good bones. No sagging on either the roofline or the porch's roofline. The rocking chair was exactly where it had been when she walked by the house a few days ago. When she'd been planning her run.

She sighed. She was going to pay for her lack of exercise.

A tarnished brass knocker was fitted to the massive oak door. Without hesitating, Amanda grasped the knocker and knocked three times firmly.

The sound cut sharply through the trilling of the birds. After a moment, the birds resumed their singing. In the distance, she could hear laughter and voices from the other side of the point.

"Maybe she's in back," said Amanda. Uncertainty now replaced determination on her face. "Maybe we should come back—"

The door opened with a creak of under-oiled hinges and they both turned to find a tall woman staring at them.

"Yes?" she asked politely. She coughed slightly, as if the word had irritated her throat on its way out.

Probably doesn't talk to many people on any given day, thought Kate.

"Hello," said Amanda, drawing the woman's attention. "My name is Amanda and this is my aunt Kate. We're staying at the cottage next door."

Mrs. Olafson was definitely of an age with Mrs. Petterson, but where Mrs. Petterson was rounded and softly wrinkled, this woman was all angles. She wore a pair of soft grey cotton trousers that had probably been in style thirty years ago, and a man's navy, cabled sweater over a white shirt. The effect reminded Kate of Katherine Hepburn, right up to the frizzy white hair in a poufy bun.

"Very nice to make your acquaintance," said Mrs. Olafson, staring at Amanda. "How can I help you?"

Kate was suddenly reminded of her mother, who at seventy-eight never let an unkind word cross her lips and was always faultlessly polite. There the resemblance ended, however. Where Mrs. Olafson was tall and gaunt, Mom was short and round, like Kate and Rose, and would no sooner have worn Dad's old shirt than she would have left dirty dishes in the sink.

"We made some chocolate chip cookies," said Amanda, holding out the tin. She smiled at the woman. "We thought we'd bring some over and introduce ourselves."

The woman's study of Amanda was beginning to unnerve Kate, though it didn't seem to bother Amanda. As though realizing she was being rude, Mrs. Olafson suddenly tore her gaze away from Amanda and smiled at Kate.

"How do you do," she said formally. "I'm Sula Olafson. Why don't you come in? I'll put on a pot of tea." She turned away and led the way into the house, clearly expecting them to follow.

Kate and Amanda glanced at each other. Who knew it would be that easy?

They followed Sula Olafson down a long, dark, wood-panelled hallway. There were three doors along the hallway, one of which was partly open. Kate glanced in as she walked by. A bedroom with a single bed, neatly made, a bookshelf, and a rocking chair. Kate had expected to see a staircase in the front hall but there was none.

Mrs. Olafson led them to the back of the house, where sunlight spilled into a large, linoleum-tiled kitchen. Kate blinked at the contrast between the dark hallway and the bright kitchen.

A scarred, sturdy rectangular pine table with wooden chairs filled half the room. Counters covered in Arborite so old it was worn through in spots followed three of the four walls. Faded green gingham curtains hung at the window over the worn apron sink. Even the toaster on the counter looked as if it had been ordered from the 1956 Eaton's catalog.

"Why don't you step through to the porch, dear," said Mrs. Olafson, looking at Kate. "Your niece can help me with the tea." She pointed to the sliding glass doors, which looked like they were relics from the seventies, even though they were the newest things in the room.

Kate hesitated. She didn't want to leave Amanda alone with the woman. Amanda looked at her and nodded slightly and Kate almost sighed in frustration. Nor did she want to make a big deal out of what was probably an innocent request.

"Of course," she said finally. She walked past a wood stove and the afghan-covered easy chair next to it, noting the hardcover book with a bookmark sticking out sitting on the seat. She wanted to read the cover of the book, but it would have been too obvious. Instead, she slid the door open and stepped onto the back porch.

She glanced back, but Mrs. Olafson and Amanda were busy filling a kettle and placing cookies on a plate. Their heads kept turning toward each other, as if wanting to keep each other in sight, and their bodies leaned toward each other. It was a curiously intimate gesture for two women who had just met.

The back porch was in shade, too, but the morning was quickly warming up. Like the front porch, this one was covered by a roof, part of which formed the floor of the upstairs balcony, if she remembered correctly. This porch needed refreshing, too, but it was clearly more used than the one at the front of the house. A wicker rocking chair with a flowered cushion on the seat sat by the door, with a matching, small round table next to it. A railing ran around the porch, breaking only for the stairs that led to the overgrown lawn, and rickety flower boxes hung over the railing at regular intervals along both sides of the stairs. By the looks of the dried-out soil in them, there hadn't been fresh flowers in the boxes for decades.

Standing next to the wicker rocking chair, Kate kept the two women in sight, following their progress. Mrs. Olafson was pouring hot water into the tea pot.

Kate glanced over the yard. If she ignored the state of the porch, not to mention the weed-choked, overgrown lawn, Mrs. Olafson had an amazing view. Like the lawn at the cottage Kate was renting, Mrs. Olafson's lawn ended at shrubs and long grasses, but they did nothing to obstruct the view of the lake shimmering in the morning light.

But still... how could she sit in the chair day in and day out and ignore the state of that yard? The porch?

Amanda came out carrying a tray with a china teapot covered in roses, matching cups and saucers, and sugar and cream bowls. She stopped as she caught sight of the yard then glanced at Kate, who shrugged.

"I'll just set this on the table," said Amanda, calling over her shoulder.

Mrs. Olafson followed behind her with a plate—with matching flowers—of cookies. "Oh dear," she said. "I should bring out more chairs. I don't often get company."

"I can do that," said Kate quickly when the woman turned back toward the door.

Kate went inside, grabbed two of the wooden chairs, which were much heavier than they looked, and headed back outside. Moments later, they were all seated with a cup of tea in hand.

"How long are you staying at the cottage?" asked Mrs. Olafson.

"We're leaving today," said Kate.

The old woman's smile faded. "I see," she murmured, glancing at Amanda. The old woman's expression was almost... possessive.

"I'm curious," said Kate abruptly and Sula Olafson and Amanda both turned to her in surprise. "On the first night I arrived," she continued, ignoring Amanda's wide-eyed look, "I saw a light climbing the side of your house, the side closest to the cottage."

Mrs. Olafson had reached for a cookie. Now she paused, cookie in hand, and cocked her head at Kate.

"How odd. What kind of light?"

Kate shrugged uncomfortably, suddenly unsure of herself. Could she be mistaken? "I'm not sure, really. I thought at first that someone was climbing the stairs to the second floor, carrying a candle."

Sula Olafson just stared at her, her pale eyes troubled. "There are no outside stairs," she said slowly.

Amanda frowned fiercely at Kate.

"Well, it was probably a reflection from the upstairs window," Kate said, wishing now she hadn't said anything. She took a sip of tea out of politeness.

Mrs. Olafson shook her head. "The upstairs is closed off."

Kate waited for more but the old woman just stared at her. When she didn't add anything, Kate smiled. "It's a big house for one person," she said invitingly. "I expect you've no need for the upstairs."

Mrs. Olafson looked down at her lap, hiding her eyes from scrutiny and suddenly, Kate felt awful.

If looks could kill, Amanda's would certainly have maimed.

"Please," Amanda said gently, laying a hand on the old woman's arm. "Try a cookie."

Mrs. Olafson looked up at her and smiled. She took a bite of the cookie and smiled. "Real butter," she said. "These are lovely." She looked at Kate.

"Oh, don't look at me," said Kate quickly. "Amanda is the chef in the family."

Amanda and Mrs. Olafson shared another smile, and something in that smile unsettled Kate.

"Sarah was a good cook, too," said Mrs. Olafson, her gaze fixed on Amanda. "You remind me of her."

The breeze kicked up just then, blowing cool over Kate's shoulders and back.

"Is Sarah your sister?" she asked, though she knew better.

"My daughter," said Mrs. Olafson, turning her attention to Kate.

"Does she live with you?" Kate caught Amanda's displeased look but ignored it.

A shadow crossed Mrs. Olafson's face, as if a cloud had covered her own personal sun. "No. Not for a long time now," she said sadly. Then she brightened. "But she's coming back."

Kate struggled to keep an expression of pleasant interest on her face. Coming back? According to Mrs. Petterson, Sula Olafson had last seen her daughter and son sometime in 1985. Now she was coming back? After no word for over twenty-five years?

"That's wonderful," said Amanda. She leaned over to refill the old woman's cup. "Where has she been?"

"I don't know," said Mrs. Olafson. She blinked rapidly, as if trying to contain tears. Her eyes were a pale blue with a dark rim around the iris.

The old woman looked past the back yard and her gaze settled on the glinting waters of the lake. Her shallow breathing finally slowed and deepened, as if the sight calmed her.

This woman spends way too much time on her own, thought

Kate. She glanced at Amanda but found her staring at Sula Olafson with tears in her eyes. Dear Lord. Maybe it was a mistake to have come here. Amanda seemed to have bonded with the old woman, and that didn't feel healthy.

Still, she was here now, and this might be her only opportunity to get some information out of the old woman.

"Is she your only child?" she asked casually. She sipped the tea and tried not to make a face at the insipid stuff. Why did people even bother with tea? Might as well drink warm dishwater.

Mrs. Olafson's face grew still and her gaze dropped to the perfectly steady cup in her hand. She remained silent for so long that Amanda shot Kate an uncertain look. Then Mrs. Olafson took a sip of her tea and shook her head.

"I have a son, too," she said quietly. "Daniel."

The silence grew uncomfortably until Kate decided to go for broke.

"Is Daniel coming back, too?"

Mrs. Olafson looked up at Kate and for as long as she lived, Kate would never forget the bleak look on the woman's face.

"I hope not," she said. "Oh, I hope not."

CHAPTER 10

KATE AND Amanda drove back to Mendenhall in their respective cars, following each other. The weather, which had been warm and sunny in Gimli, grew cloudier and cooler as they drove past Winnipeg.

Kate made a mental note to call Bert and tell him of their change of plans. And the bakery in Gimli. She couldn't help but feel she had failed Amanda. The holiday that had been meant to raise her niece's spirits had turned into a disaster that had almost cost the girl her life. Going back home was the right move, she was firmly convinced of that, but nothing had been solved. She still didn't know what was going on with Amanda.

Maybe Amanda felt she had made a mistake moving to Mendenhall. Maybe she missed the hustle and bustle of working and living in Old Montreal. Mendenhall was certainly quieter than Montreal. Amanda had even mentioned moving to Winnipeg. But her business in Mendenhall seemed to be going well, and she and Trepalli were definitely an "item," so what was bothering the girl?

Dammitall. She was going to have to talk to Rose. Rose might know what was up, or at least she might know how to get the information out of the girl.

For an experienced interrogator, you're sure no good when it comes to family, she told herself glumly.

But she knew better than to take the direct approach again. Amanda was just like her mother in that respect. She would keep denying that anything was wrong and pretty soon, she would start avoiding Kate.

The first drops of rain hit the windshield as she entered the outskirts of Mendenhall. The wind had picked up, rustling the fields of canola and sunflowers. The sunflowers were starting to open up. Another week and they would present their round brown faces to the sun and follow its progress all day long. The air coming through the vents smelled of wet, hot pavement and sweet clover, and Kate breathed deeply, trying to ease the stress from her shoulders.

She sighed and slowed her speed to follow the posted limit. She had wanted to follow Amanda home and make sure she was all right, but Amanda had given her a look and told her to please stop worrying and go check on the station, since she knew that's what Kate wanted to do.

In the brief hour they had spent with Sula Olafson, Kate had grown convinced that the old woman was a little "tetched," as Mom would say. It wasn't so much what the woman said as the way she looked at Amanda and how she spoke to her. She kept touching Amanda, as if to make sure she was really there. Kate might as well not have been there at all.

When Kate had finally gotten up to leave, both Sula Olafson and Amanda had looked at her in dismay.

"We need to get going," Kate had said firmly. "We have a long drive ahead of us."

"You're leaving?" Sula had asked in alarm. She'd struggled out of her wicker chair as Amanda slowly got up. "But you've only just arrived!"

Kate had looked at the two distraught faces before her and her heart had sunk a little. They both had tears in their eyes. Time to get out of here.

She had held firm, and by the time they finished packing

up their cars, Amanda had returned to her normal self. But the episode had spooked Kate and she was glad to see the last of Stony Point and Gimli.

She'd lost track of the days but thought it might be Tuesday. Or maybe Wednesday. It didn't help that she hadn't slept last night.

There wasn't much traffic on the highway and soon she flashed her headlights at Amanda to indicate she was taking the turnoff to downtown. Amanda stuck her arm out the window and waved. She would take the next exit, which would get her home more quickly.

But instead of turning off on Mendenhall Drive to go to the station, Kate kept driving down Main Street, toward her house. She finally turned onto her street but only far enough to make sure Amanda's Tercel was in the drive. Then she turned around and drove to the station.

It was silly, but she'd wanted to make sure the girl had actually gone home, and not turned around to head back to Gimli.

Ten minutes later, she drove into the parking lot of the Mendenhall Police Station. All the patrol cars were out, she noted with approval. She had instituted a policy that constables should park their private vehicles at the back, leaving the few parking spots at the front for visitors. Only she and DC McKell had designated parking spots at the front, and Kate didn't feel guilty about it. Not one little bit.

One disadvantage of the new policy was that she couldn't tell who was on duty without driving around the detachment. She glanced at her dashboard clock. Just past two o'clock. Martins wouldn't be on duty; he'd been on last night. No wait—he'd been on days. Until seven o'clock. So he should still be on, right?

She parked and got out of the car. Rain drops fell on her head, shoulders, and chest and she hurried to the stoop. She didn't plan to be at the station long. Well, not very long, anyway. The window on the screen door was open, letting in the rain, and the door slammed behind her when she walked in. She paused to slide the window down before heading into the duty room. She glanced at the duty desk when she passed by but no one was sitting at it. When she entered, however, she found Rob McKell and Martins standing in the middle of the duty room, arms crossed over their chests, staring at her. She stopped in the doorway and looked at them uncertainly.

"Gentlemen," she said.

"Chief," said Martins disapprovingly. His crinkly red hair looked frizzy with the humidity. He was holding a clipboard and a pen.

"You're supposed to be on holidays," said McKell sternly.

She shrugged. "I am. I just dropped by for a quick visit."

McKell uncrossed his arms and spread them wide. Before he could say what was on his mind, she put up a hand.

"Why don't you join me in my office and brief me on these fires," she said.

His mouth closed, as did his expression, and worry slammed into Kate with the force of a punch. She turned and walked to her office in the far corner, next to the locker room. Her sandals squeaked on the linoleum floor.

She went around her desk and leaned down to turn on the computer before sitting down. McKell entered behind her and stood leaning against the door jamb.

"So," he started. "Why are you back so early?"

She stifled a sigh. Clearly he wanted to work his way up to what was really bothering him.

McKell had turned out to be a good deputy chief, once they worked out their initial problems. But he did feel a little too pro-prietary about the job sometimes. He probably thought her early return reflected a lack of trust in him. If he knew how tired and grumpy she was, he'd be more careful. Or maybe not. This was McKell, after all.

"DC, I hope you're not about to give me heck, because that would be a little like the pot calling the kettle black."

McKell, who had opened his mouth, closed it suddenly and

a faint pink tinged his cheeks. He grinned at her sheepishly. "All right. You got me." He crossed his arms again and looked at her, studying her face. Once again she found herself thinking that he was a good-looking man, despite his receding hairline. Sure, he was big and fit, but it was those clear blue eyes of his that made him so attractive. He always looked at you like there was nothing else worth looking at. No wonder the guy had been married three times.

"You look like hell," he said, instantly dispelling the warmth she'd been feeling toward him.

She raised an eyebrow at him. "Stop it with the charm," she said. "You'll make me blush."

He laughed and uncrossed his arms, dropping easily into one of the two visitor chairs. "What exactly didn't work out?" he asked. "Even I enjoy going to Gimli."

Kate sighed and sat back. She really wanted a coffee. "Let's just say it wasn't the restful break I was hoping for."

Something in her tone gave him pause and when he spoke again, he was serious.

"Everything okay? Amanda?"

She glanced at him quickly, then away. She should have known that McKell would pick up on her unease about Amanda. She shrugged. "She wasn't enjoying it, either," she said. "Now, where's Charlotte?"

"I let her go early," said McKell. "Her guy is in town for a few days."

Kate nodded. Charlotte Hrebien, the station's only administrative support, was supposed to work from seven o'clock to three o'clock, but she often worked late and refused to claim overtime. She understood the stress on the detachment's budget as well as Kate did. So when Josh, her new boyfriend, an itinerant veterinarian out of Winnipeg, was in the area, McKell and Kate conspired to give the girl time off.

"So, what's happening with the fires?"

He passed a hand over his face and sighed, and for the first time, Kate saw the signs of fatigue: shadowed eyes, deep grooves on either side of his mouth, and a tightness in his shoulders. She braced herself.

"Looks like arson," he said. "At least the first one, at the hardware store."

Kate leaned back and listened quietly as he reported.

The fire in the alley behind Brockman's had been started with oil-soaked rags. Only dumb luck had kept the fire from destroying Brockman's and the adjoining stores. The only witnesses were a couple returning home from a birthday party at one in the morning. They hadn't seen anyone in the alley. The second fire, yesterday at the café, had started in the kitchen over lunch. That one was still being investigated.

When he stopped, she nodded.

"What about Brockman's fired employee? Did you question him?"

McKell sighed. "He was still drunk as a skunk when we picked him up. Says he can't remember a damned thing from the night of the fire. We're traced his movements from the time he was fired to about eleven o'clock that night. He went to the Cave and stayed there until shortly before eleven. Then one of his buddies gave him a ride home. Buddy confirms it."

"Eleven," mused Kate. "That still gives him ample time to get to Brockman's and light the fire."

McKell looked skeptical. "Maybe. Theoretically. But by all accounts, the guy was too drunk to make it out of the bar on his own. I doubt he would have been able to get behind the wheel and drive downtown, let alone light the fire without setting himself on fire."

Kate let it go for now. The guy might have been putting on an act to give himself an alibi. Even a blood test would have been inconclusive, since it wouldn't prove when he had taken the drinks.

McKell shrugged as if he had read her thoughts. "Fire marshal is still investigating the café fire, but honestly, it looks like stupidity more than arson. Someone left a dishcloth too close to the grill and by the time they noticed, the whole wall was in flames."

Kate's eyebrows rose. "That's a pretty small kitchen," she said. "How did they not notice a fire?"

"Everyone was out front," explained McKell. "They were short-staffed that day and the cook was serving, too."

"Who's investigating?"

"Ray Evans," said McKell. "He was already in town investigating the hardware store fire."

"Patrols...?"

"I've ordered extra patrols of the downtown area."

Kate barely stifled a yawn. "All right," she said. "Not much else we can do until we get Evans' report. Now, what about our panty raider?"

McKell shook his head. "He's moved out of our jurisdiction. Last report puts him in Sidney." He put a hand up to forestall her. "I've PIPped it," he said, meaning he'd submitted the information to the Police Information Portal, "and personally called the municipalities to the east. I let Bert know, too."

"Okay." She reminded herself to call Bert as soon as she could. "Did anyone check with Brandon or Virden?"

McKell gave her the raised eyebrow look, the one that said, *Of course I checked. Do you think I'm stupid?* But he contented himself with, "Yep. Brandon had one case of stolen underwear. Nothing in Virden."

Kate nodded in silent acknowledgement. She was glad the panty raider slash rapist-in-training was out of her jurisdiction, but she didn't like the fact that no one knew who he was. Or where he was. At the rate he was going, he'd be raping before he hit Winnipeg.

"All right," she said. "Someone will eventually apprehend him."

"Yes," agreed McKell. "I just hope it's *before* he hurts a girl."

They looked at each other in silence for a few seconds, then the good DC got up and left, leaving her to her emails.

* * *

An hour later, she was done with her email and had logged on to CPIC, the Canadian Police Information Centre, to check out outstanding warrants and warnings. She saw McKell's advisory on the panty raider—time to find a different name for him, she told herself sternly. "Panty raider" made him sound like a kid on a lark. This guy wasn't on a lark. Not if he was assaulting young girls. But she couldn't call him "Unknown Subject" or "Unsub"—that was too much like a television show.

She sighed and it turned into another yawn. She glanced at the time at the bottom of the screen. Four-thirty. Her stomach rumbled, reminding her that she hadn't had anything to eat since the chocolate chip cookies that morning. Time to go home.

She was about to log out and shut down the computer when she remembered that she had wanted to do a little digging around Sula Olafson and her children. She could do it from home, of course, but it was probably better to do it where Amanda wasn't.

Another yawn caught her by surprise and she decided to get a coffee first. Martins was alone in the duty room when she walked out. He was typing at the duty desk computer, his hunt-and-peck method surprisingly fast.

"Coffee?" said Kate as she walked into the hallway.

"There's a fresh pot," said Martins absently, misunderstanding her question.

She was about to rephrase her offer when the phone rang and Martins picked it up. She headed into the lunch room and poured two cups. The rain had stopped and the open window let in the smell of wet earth and vegetation. She tried to remember if Martins liked sugar, but could only come up with a memory of him putting cream in his coffee. Taking a chance, she splashed some cream into his cup and stirred. As she passed by the duty desk, she plunked the cup down in front of him. His brown eyes crinkled up in a smile and he nodded his thanks, still talking into the phone.

The outside door opened just then and Trepalli walked in, wearing a frown.

"Chief," he said. "Is Amanda all right?"

Kate's eyebrows rose.

"Good afternoon, Constable," she said politely.

He blushed and she struggled not to grin. These young ones were so easy to fluster.

"Sorry, Chief," he said in embarrassment. "How are you?"

"I'm fine," she said, relenting. She headed toward her office. "And Amanda's fine, too. We just came home early."

She glanced over her shoulder at him before re-entering her office. He stood in the middle of the duty room, having trailed after her, a tall, lean boy with a good build, thick dark hair, and truly gorgeous blue eyes. Those blue eyes stared at her as if he were trying to tell her something. She closed the door, only then registering the circles under his eyes. He'd looked a little thinner than the last time she had seen him, too.

Hmm.

Something was clearly keeping the boy up. Was it the same something that was keeping Amanda from sleeping well?

Her heart sank a little. Despite his good looks and the fact that he knew he was good-looking, Trepalli was a good cop. She had been worried when he and Amanda started seeing each other, but it was really none of her business, as long as it didn't affect his work. And as long as he didn't hurt her.

And if she were to be truly honest with herself, she'd admit to a fondness for the boy.

Stay out of it, she told herself firmly. *It's none of your business.*

Except that she couldn't get the stricken look on his face out of her mind.

Oh, for Pete's sake. She shook her head. *Stop it. You're starting to act like Mom.*

CHAPTER 11

THE SMELL that greeted her when she walked through the door almost made her drool.

"Just in time," called Amanda from the kitchen. "Dinner's almost on."

Kate dropped her keys in the basket on the small entryway table and set her tote bag on the floor by the hallway. She would unpack later.

"What smells so good?" she asked as she entered the kitchen.

As usual, the kitchen looked as if a hurricane had blown through it. Kate had come to accept the mess as the price of eating like a queen.

"Fettuccini Alfredo," said Amanda, not taking her attention from the sauce she was stirring. "Go sit outside. I set the table on the deck."

Kate took a detour to drop the tote bag in her bedroom. In the end, she had given up on the idea of digging more deeply into Sula Olafson and her family. At least for the moment. Seeing Trepalli had put her off staying at the station.

She washed her hands before walking through the dining room to the French doors. She stepped out onto the deck and sighed with pleasure. The deck surface was still damp from the rain earlier in the day, and the smell of wet wood mingled with the fresh scent of damp soil and growing grass. She loved the prairie light at this time of day. Low and golden, as if magic hovered in the air. She walked down the steps to the grass, ignoring the fact that her feet were getting wet, and went to the edge of her property, which dropped off precipitously in a cliff that stepped down into another cliff until the Mendenhall valley spread before her. Beyond the town were fields of wheat, canola, and sunflowers, all shimmering like a promise.

She couldn't actually see the station but she could see the large loop of Mendenhall Drive and the straight arrow of Main Street bisecting it. Long shadows softened the contours of buildings until it seemed as if Mendenhall was a mirage conjured out of her tired brain.

She took a deep breath. Wild roses mixed with sweet clover. Could anything, anywhere, smell more inviting?

"Here we are." Amanda came out of the kitchen door carrying a tray and stood looking around for a moment before she found Kate. "Come sit."

Not needing another invitation, Kate joined her niece at the patio table. Amanda had wiped it down and already set it with place mats, cutlery, and real napkins. There were even wine glasses and an open bottle of Chardonnay with a napkin covering the opening. The salad bowl was also waiting with a plate covering it against the investigations of insects.

Amanda set the tray down and placed the plates of creamy pasta with generous heapings of bacon on the table. Kate sat at her regular spot, facing the back yard, and Amanda ground fresh pepper over the pasta before sitting down, too.

When she first arrived in Mendenhall, Amanda had been horrified at the fact that Kate would salt her food before even tasting it. It had taken her a while, but Kate had finally come around to Amanda's reasoning. She found that she rarely needed salt anymore.

She poured the golden wine into their glasses and they silently toasted each other before digging into the food. Kate surreptitiously watched her niece eat. She seemed normal, but there was a tautness about her, as if she couldn't fully relax.

"This is delicious," Kate said finally. "Is that basil in the salad?"

Amanda nodded and gave Kate a proud smile, as if Kate were a child who had proven an apt pupil. And to be honest, Kate had learned a lot about food since Amanda had moved in. She sighed.

"What?" asked Amanda.

"I haven't gone for a run in days," said Kate. "I am not looking forward to my next one."

Amanda grinned. "You're on holidays," she said. "Give yourself a break."

Right. Tell that to my hips.

She was about to say it out loud when through the open French doors they heard a knocking at the front door. Kate made to get up, but Amanda was closer and waved her back.

"I'll get it," she said.

Kate twirled another forkful of the *al dente* pasta and put it in her mouth. Good lord, the child could cook.

She heard the sound of voices coming from the front entryway and waited to see if Amanda would call her. Since her niece had moved in, she'd had much more company at the house. In spite of her crammed schedule, Amanda still found time to make friends. For some reason, they seemed to like coming to the house.

"You're being ridiculous."

Kate stopped with her wine glass halfway to her lips. That was Trepalli's voice. He sounded angry.

"Really?" Amanda's voice rose. "I'm glad you take my concerns so seriously."

Uh oh. Kate slowly placed the wine glass back on the table and glanced through the French doors at the dining room. She couldn't see the front entrance from her vantage point but their voices floated through clearly. Too clearly.

She quietly pushed her chair back and stood up, glancing at her watch as she did. Seven-thirty. Well, he was off shift, anyway. Must have come over straight from the station. She pulled the doors closed quietly then glanced at the remaining food on the table. So much for that. She placed napkins over both plates and went down the steps into to the yard.

When she was safely distanced from the house, she looked back at it. Despite the fact that it was still daylight, there was a light on in the kitchen where Amanda had been working. Since her niece had moved in, the kitchen light was always on and the house was always filled with wonderful smells. Amanda would often have her iPod hooked up to speakers and would play her opera music full blast, singing along with the divas, despite the fact that really, she couldn't sing.

Most nights, Kate would come home to a warm house, good food, and family.

She had bought the house because of the view, but it had taken Amanda to turn it into a home.

To her surprise, tears pricked her eyes. She hadn't realized how stressful it had been to see Amanda unhappy. Now that she knew Trepalli was the cause, she felt anger stirring in her. That boy. It was one thing to charm all the girls in town—heck, in Brandon and Winnipeg, too—but it took a constable with a death wish to put the moves on the chief of police's niece and then break her heart.

What the hell was he thinking?

She had taken a step toward the house, having convinced herself to give Trepalli a piece of her mind, when her cell phone rumbled in the back pocket of her pedal pushers. She jumped and fished it out. It was Bert.

"Hi," she said, once she had thumbed it on.

"Hi yourself," replied Bert and she immediately felt better on hearing his voice. "How's the holiday?"

She sighed and turned her back on the house. "We came back early." She told him about the nightly crying, about Amanda's sleepwalking, and about meeting Mrs. Olafson.

"Sounds like one weird holiday."

"Yep," agreed Kate. "But I think I figured out what's been bothering Amanda lately."

"Oh?"

"Trepalli."

"What's he done?" demanded Bert, immediately protective. Kate smiled at the phone.

"I don't know," she admitted. "He's in the house right now, arguing with her."

"Where are *you*?" he asked, puzzled.

"In the yard. We were having dinner when he arrived. I thought I'd give them some privacy but honestly, I feel like marching in there and giving him a piece of my mind."

"Katie, you should let them work it out," warned Bert. "You'll only make it worse if you interfere."

"That's my niece he's hurting," she said.

"You don't know what happened," Bert pointed out. "For all you know, Amanda did something to *him*."

Kate pulled the phone away from her ear and stared at it for a second before bringing it back. "This is Trepalli we're talking about, the romantic scourge of southern Manitoba."

"Well, Amanda's no slouch, either," Bert pointed out. "I'm sure she has lots of guys sniffing around her."

"She's not a bitch in heat, you know," said Kate sharply. Where did he get off talking about Amanda like that?

"Don't be ridiculous," said Bert and she felt a sudden spike of irritation. That was exactly what Trepalli had said, in exactly the same tone of voice.

She opened her mouth to reply sharply when she stopped and looked around. The arm holding the phone dropped to her side, even though she could hear Bert talking at the other end. She turned in a circle, trying to find what was wrong, what had triggered the sudden adrenaline in her system. Then she smelled it.

Everything stilled around her as she focused on the Mendenhall valley, and the cluster of businesses and streets in the down-town core, and the flames shooting so high into the air that they could be seen from a mile away.

She turned and ran for the house.

CHAPTER 12

"THEY'RE STARTING to disperse, Chief."

Kate looked around. Tourmeline still had the camera to his eye, filming the crowd of lookie-loos. She had tasked him with documenting the fire and the surroundings, including the onlookers. Trepalli had been doing the same thing but with a digital camera. She knew of at least three arson cases where the arsonist had been identified in the crowd.

And three fires in three days, all in the downtown area? The hardware store, the café, and now the coffee shop and comic store. It was arson.

The fire had died down under the onslaught of the fire hoses. A dozen firefighters, both professional and volunteer, had responded to the fire alarm by the time Kate arrived downtown, Trepalli following behind her. She'd left Amanda standing forlornly in the doorway with a promise to call as soon as she could.

She heard McKell ordering someone to stay back and looked around. Tourmeline was right. The crowd was dispersing. She and McKell had been busy in the first half hour, setting up road blocks and controlling the crowd, but this was essentially Fire Chief Avramson's show.

She shivered and wished she had taken her jacket from the car. But it had still been daylight and warm when she arrived. The clouds had dispersed, leaving the sun shining, and with the fire blazing, it had been too warm. Now it was past ten o'clock and the temperature was falling. It didn't help that her sandaled feet were soaked from all the water thrown at the fire.

"Reporters are here."

Kate jumped and turned to find McKell staring at the caved-in roof of the comic book store. It was attached to the destroyed coffee shop, and while the flames had been kept from the store, it had suffered a great deal of smoke and water damage. Not to mention the roof.

"Did you speak to them?"

He shook his head. "Just to say we were here to support the fire department."

Kate nodded. The last thing she needed was to have anyone in her department interviewed, instead of Avramson. Things had been touchy between the two departments ever since the emergency exercises last winter, when they had come across a real body and Kate had had to cancel the exercise.

She sighed. She would eventually have to patch things up with the fire chief, but honestly, he could be such an ass.

She had already determined a rough timeline. Both businesses were closed by the time the flames had broken out, but not by long. Kate had seen the flames at around seven-thirty, and the coffee shop had closed at six, at the same time as the comic book store, with the last employee out by seven.

"Are we sure there was no one inside?" she asked. McKell was still in uniform, even though he was off duty when the call came in. Kate sometimes thought he didn't own civilian clothes. Maybe he just liked the way he looked in his uniform.

"Fire Hall despatcher contacted the buildings' owners," said McKell, finally looking at her. Manitoba Hydro had cut electricity to the block and they were lit only by the streetlights of the adjacent blocks. The faint light gave McKell a mysterious look, hiding his eyes in shadow. "They're busy contacting their tenants."

Kate looked down at her cold, sandaled feet. The comic book store and the coffee shop shared a wall, and each building had a second story with offices rented out. It would take a while to contact each tenant and make sure no one had been working. Even then, it would take a physical search to determine for sure no one had been trapped in the fire. She didn't envy Chief Avramson.

She wished she could interview the owners to ask if they had noticed anyone loitering around their shops, but it wasn't her purview. Avramson and Evans, the fire marshal, would be investigating the arson case. She and her constables were only playing a supporting role, she kept reminding herself.

If the fire marshal determined that it was arson, however, then it would be up to her to investigate. She made a mental note to ask Albertson to get the list of tenants from the owners. Maybe one of them had seen something.

"It's gotta be arson," said Tourmeline, coming toward them. He had flipped his camera closed and was zipping it into its case. He looked up. "Don't you think?"

Kate and McKell shrugged in unison. She was pretty sure McKell believed it was arson, just like her, but they were both too experienced to prejudge a case. Out loud, anyway.

"We'll have to wait for the arson investigation," said McKell.

"Who was on patrol?" asked Kate.

"Nobody," said Tourmeline promptly. "It was shift change. We had just finished inspecting our vehicles and were heading out for our first patrol when we heard the sirens and got the call from Albertson. By then we were on Main Street and could see the flames."

Kate and McKell glanced at each other.

"Either that's one lucky arsonist," said McKell grimly, "or he timed it just right."

"I don't believe in luck," said Kate. They had to find this guy before he killed someone.

* * *

Kate assigned Fallon and Oppenheimer to guard the scene.

Then she, Tourmeline, McKell, Boychuk, and Trepalli headed back to the station. The fire marshal wouldn't be able to examine the scene until daylight, and until the remains of the building cooled down. In the meantime, she wanted to see Tourmeline's footage, and download Trepalli's photos.

They all gathered in the duty room and Tourmeline downloaded the video card onto the department's internal site. It seemed to take forever, so Kate went to the lunch room and helped herself to coffee. The coffee smelled as if it had been on the burner since last week, but she leaned against the counter across from the window and sipped, hoping it would help her stay alert. There was an oak tree just outside the window, but right now all she could see was a tired, middle-aged, dishevelled woman staring back at her.

The coffee tasted as bad as it smelled. She poured the contents of her cup down the drain and made a fresh pot.

She looked up as Trepalli walked into the room, still wearing the reflective vest he had donned over his tee-shirt. His pale jeans were smudged with soot, as were his bare arms. His hair was mussed and his eyes bloodshot, and there was dark stubble on his lean cheeks and chin. Kate blinked. Even tired and dirty, he managed to look like every woman's fantasy.

"Chief." He nodded curtly and headed for the pot of coffee.

That's right, she thought. *I interrupted his fight with Amanda.* Amanda!

With a sigh she set her cup down on the counter, but even as she dug through her pedal pusher pocket she knew the cell phone wasn't there. Where the hell had she left it?

She headed back toward her office and the land line.

"Got it," said Tourmeline as she re-entered the duty room. He looked up at her and grinned, clearly pleased with himself. Kate couldn't help but grin back. The technically-challenged had to stick together, after all. Boychuk rolled his eyes and was about to say something when the phone rang and Albertson raised a hand to order silence.

"Mendenhall Police Department," he said. As they all waited for him to finish dealing with the call, Kate decided that Charlotte was right. They really needed to get one of those cordless clip-things so that the duty officer wouldn't have to be chained to the desk.

As Albertson finished dealing with the call, McKell emerged from his office, still looking as fresh as when she'd first seen him that afternoon. He handed her a piece of paper.

"The tenants above both stores," he said in a quiet voice. "There's a dozen of them."

Kate looked the question at him, but he shook his head. "I don't know," he said. "The landlords haven't been able to reach them all yet."

She nodded jerkily just as Albertson hung up.

"All right," she told Tourmeline and he blinked those brown deer-in-the-headlight eyes and clicked the mouse. They all leaned in toward the flat screen.

"Turn it up," said McKell as they strained to hear the sound from the computer's speakers. Albertson reached over Tourmeline's shoulder and turned on the auxiliary speakers. The room filled with the noise of men shouting orders and horns honking and water shooting out of hoses under pressure. But above it all, like the soundtrack to a horror movie, the roaring of the fire.

Kate had thought the video would be dark, but the fire cast a flickering, warm glow over everything. Her heart started pounding faster as she saw the front window of the coffee shop explode from the heat of the fire within. They followed Tourmeline as he walked a wide circuit around the block, filming at a wide angle and occasionally zooming in when something caught his eye.

"This is the alley," said Tourmeline from the speakers, and they all jumped, even the real-time Tourmeline. "Garbage pickup was yesterday," continued the voice behind the camera, "so there shouldn't be much in the dumpster."

A mug of coffee suddenly appeared in front of her and Kate blinked in surprise. Trepalli looked at her steadily and she accepted the cup from him with a nod before turning back to the screen.

Next to her, Boychuk, Tourmeline's usual partner, smelled of a light, spicy aftershave, under the pervasive smell of smoke. He smelled good, another contradiction in a man full of them. With his pouchy eyes and rumpled uniform, he always looked like he had just rolled out of bed after sleeping in his clothes. But she knew that Eeyore exterior hid a keen, observant mind. Now she looked at him, wondering why he hadn't been with his partner, and he shrugged, reading her mind. "I was out front," he explained. "Helping with crowd control." He nodded toward the image on the screen. "Besides, he wasn't alone."

He was right.

Light suddenly blinded the camera and it dipped away, as if Tourmeline had turned away. "The pumper truck," explained Tourmeline next to her. After a moment, the camera picked up movements as Tourmeline approached the back of the burning coffee shop, and Kate finally made out half a dozen firefighters swarming over the alley behind the buildings. The smaller of the fire station's two fire engines was wedged in the alley, providing light and giving the firefighters access to water to hose down the back of the two buildings as well as the buildings across the alley. The view shifted to the blackened walls and the broken windows on the second floor.

The image suddenly veered wildly as the camera swung down and Kate closed her eyes against the sudden vertigo. A grating sound caused her to open them again and she saw the interior of the dumpster container. A couple of flat boxes, like the kind that held cans of soup, some clear plastic, and that was all.

"Nothing here," confirmed Tourmeline's voice. The camera swooped again, and for a moment she was staring at the night sky, then the camera was level and Tourmeline continued to film.

The telephone rang again and Tourmeline paused the video while Albertson answered. They all listened as he explained to the mayor that the chief was out of the office right now but he would have her call back as soon as she returned. He cut the connection and Kate smiled at him. The last thing she wanted right now was to have to reassure the mayor when she had no information.

She nodded at Tourmeline and he started the video again. He took footage of the firefighters raining water onto the roof and walls of the buildings and she heard a soft sigh beside her. McKell. She knew exactly how he felt. All those men clomping around the alley, compromising trace and diluting any possible evidence...

Couldn't be helped.

The camera abruptly about-faced and headed back the way it had come. They all turned to look at Tourmeline.

"Pumper blocked the way," he said, not taking his gaze off the screen.

As Tourmeline had made his way back to Main Street, he had slowed and taken a long panoramic shot of the crowd gathered at the two blocked intersections. The light was uncertain, with the ladder truck, heavy rescue vehicle, and police cruisers' headlights providing stark lighting, alternating with deep shadows occasionally lit by the revolving red and white lights.

All six of them crowded around the tiny screen, trying to make out faces. Kate abruptly straightened, almost colliding with McKell's chin.

"This is ridiculous," she said. "We need a bigger screen. Is there any way to enhance the images?"

Tourmeline looked at her. "I'm sure there is, Chief, but I wouldn't know how."

"Brandon University's got a film department," said Trepalli. "I bet they could help us."

A small part of Kate wondered if there was a good-looking young woman working in the film department, but she bit her tongue.

"All right," she said. She glanced at the clock on the computer. Past eleven. "Let's call Brandon first thing. If they can't help, I'm sure somewhere in Winnipeg is a company that could help us." She looked around at the men surrounding her. They were all huddled on the small platform of the duty desk, and it was growing a little warm from the body heat. Not to mention uncomfortable. She stepped down onto the floor proper and immediately felt better.

"Trepalli, have you downloaded the pictures?" she asked.

"Yes, ma'am," he said promptly. "They're already on the computer."

"Good. You can go home," she said and realized too late that she sounded dismissive when McKell slid a sideways glance at her. "You're on duty tomorrow?"

Trepalli shook his head. "No, ma'am. On days off."

"All right." She looked at Tourmeline and Boychuk. "The firefighters are going to be on scene for the rest of the night, but I still want a police presence to make sure the barriers aren't breached. The two of you can spell Fallon and Oppenheimer. Take one-hour shifts. Report in hourly. Report any unusual activity."

Boychuk nodded but Tourmeline cleared his throat. "I could do some initial editing," he said, nodding at the computer screen they'd all been watching. "E-mailing the whole video is probably not a good idea. It'll be a huge file. I could make a copy of the crowd scene only to make it easier to email. Otherwise, we may have to drive to Brandon—or Winnipeg—with a thumb drive."

"All right," she said and Boychuk grabbed his cap from on top of the log book and headed out. Albertson resumed his seat at the duty desk and Tourmeline sat down at Charlotte's computer, the newest one in the detachment.

"Your office?" said McKell. When Kate nodded, he continued. "I'll grab a coffee." He walked out of the duty room and only then did Kate realize that Trepalli was still there.

"With your permission," he said stiffly, "I'd like to see them, too."

Kate tried to decide if her hesitation was in reaction to his obvious exhaustion or due to the fact that he had made Amanda unhappy. Finally she shrugged. The boy wanted to see the pictures right away. He could have waited until tomorrow after he'd slept, but he wanted to see them tonight.

It was the kind of thing she would have done in his place.

He followed her into her office and watched as she turned her computer screen so that he and McKell would be able to see it, too. She sat down and pulled up the file. A shiver ran up her bare arms and once again, she wished she had brought her jacket in from the car.

"Ma'am?" Trepalli's voice was tentative. "About earlier this evening..."

Kate's hand shot out, palm up, before she could stop it and he stumbled to a stop. She looked at him. "It's none of my business," she said grimly. "And this is not the time."

He took a deep breath and she couldn't tell if it was out of frustration or relief. "Yes, ma'am," he said, just as McKell arrived with his coffee.

The deputy chief looked from one to the other but wisely kept quiet.

* * *

Amanda arrived at the station ten minutes later.

Kate looked up from the screen as she heard voices out in the duty room. Trepalli's head swivelled toward the door and only then did Kate recognize Amanda's voice.

"Dammit," she muttered. "I forgot to call her."

McKell stood up and stretched. "Well, it's not like we're accomplishing anything here," he said sourly.

He was right. They'd gone through all of Trepalli's crowd shots, hoping someone would stand out, but while some faces were unfamiliar to Kate, neither Trepalli nor McKell identified anyone as a stranger.

Either the arsonist was too smart to get caught in a photograph, or he—or she—was a local. She didn't know which theory was more disturbing.

Kate stood up, too. Her stomach rumbled and she smiled. That girl had her conditioned.

"Let's see what she brought us," said McKell with an answering grin. He, too, was conditioned to associating Amanda's presence with food. Trepalli stood up to allow Kate to pass and she tried not to notice how he lagged behind as she stepped into the duty room.

Tourmeline and Albertson looked up guiltily as she and McKell entered. Each man had half a sandwich in one hand and a cookie in the other.

"There had better be more," said McKell grimly, folding his arms over his chest.

"Where's Amanda?" asked Kate at the same time.

"Right here," called Amanda, suddenly appearing in the hallway beyond the duty desk. "I put the food in the lunch..." She trailed off, her attention having caught on something behind Kate.

Kate automatically turned around to see Trepalli standing a few feet behind her. He stared at Amanda as if there was no one else in the room. Kate glanced around to see the same expression on Amanda's face.

The tableau held for a few eternal seconds, then Albertson cleared his throat, freeing everyone from their paralysis.

Trepalli headed for the hallway and the back door. "Goodnight, all."

"Goodnight, Constable," said Kate to his back. Amanda's face cleared of expression as he passed by her, then the screen door slammed shut behind him and her shoulders slumped slightly.

Albertson and Tourmeline exchanged glances.

"Are you done?" McKell asked Tourmeline gruffly.

Tourmeline blinked at him a few times before connecting the dots. "Yes, sir," he said. "I've copied it as 'crowd scene' in the same folder."

"Good. Now go spell Fallon and Oppenheimer."

"Yes, sir," said Tourmeline, scrambling to his feet. He grabbed his cap and headed for the front door. "Thanks for the goodies, Amanda," he said, waving his sandwich at her.

She smiled and nodded, but didn't move. It occurred to Kate

that Boychuk had left with the patrol car, which meant that Tourmeline was probably standing in the parking lot and calling his partner on the cell phone. Clearly he preferred waiting outside to waiting inside. She couldn't blame him.

"Well, I guess I'll head out, too," said McKell in the uncomfortable silence.

Kate nodded. "I'll be going, too," she said. "We can follow up tomorrow."

He left and the duty room seemed suddenly empty. Albertson began writing up the log at the duty desk.

Kate looked at her niece. "I just need to turn my computer off," she said. Not that Amanda needed to wait for her. After all, she had driven here in her own vehicle. Still, she was loitering with intent, which led Kate to thinking that maybe the girl wanted to talk to her. Oh joy.

She went back to her office and turned off the computer before wishing Albertson a good night and ushering Amanda out of the station. Tourmeline was gone. McKell probably gave him a ride to the arson site.

They stood in the parking lot, empty except for her Explorer and Amanda's Tercel, listening to the moths bump up against the light over the door. Kate could hear the firefighters spraying water on the dying fire six blocks away, and even from this distance, the faint acrid stink of the fire caught at her nose.

Amanda shivered, and Kate shivered in reaction, suddenly reminded that she, too, was only wearing a tee-shirt.

"Why did you come?" she finally asked her niece.

"You didn't call," said Amanda, and there was a note of defensiveness in her voice. "I wanted to make sure you were all right."

Kate opened her mouth only to close it. Amanda could easily have called the station. Albertson would have filled her in. She had wanted to come, and not because of Kate.

Oh lord. She really didn't want to hear about what Trepalli had done to make her niece so unhappy. Because then Kate might have to kill him.

"I did some research," said Amanda.

Kate blinked in confusion. Research about Trepalli?

Amanda rubbed her arms and looked up at the night sky. Unlike the one at the cottage, this sky hid its stars behind a white-wash of light pollution.

"On what?" asked Kate cautiously. She pulled her car keys out of her pocket and clicked her driver door unlocked.

"The Olafsons."

Kate's hand dropped to her side and she turned to look at her niece.

"What kind of research?"

Amanda shrugged. "Anything I could find. Did you know that Sula's family owned a lumber mill in the fifties and sixties? That's how they made their money. Sula married a Bergstrom but kept the Olafson name. Her children had their father's name."

Kate's eyebrows rose. "You got all that on a Google search?"

Amanda's smile slashed the night before disappearing. "And on a genealogical site for the province. A lot of newspapers are digit-izing their archives, too."

That's my niece, thought Kate proudly. *She would have made a good investigator.*

"What is it about that woman?" she asked suddenly. "The two of you were acting like you'd always known each other."

Amanda frowned a little as she considered. "It *does* feel like I've always known her. She kind of reminds me of Mom."

Kate's eyebrows rose. Sula Olafson was nothing like Rose. Physically or otherwise.

"Besides," continued Amanda, "don't you feel sorry for her? I keep wondering how Mom would feel if I had run away and she never heard from me again."

She's identifying with Sarah Bergstrom, Kate suddenly realized. It was as if Amanda didn't realize that today Sarah would be close to Kate's age, not the young woman who had left so many years ago.

"They may well have had a good reason to leave," she said slowly. No matter how inoffensive Sula Olafson appeared today, maybe she had been a tyrant to her children.

But Amanda shook her head firmly. "No. It was all him. Sarah wouldn't have left her mother if not for Daniel."

Well, for Pete's sake. Amanda couldn't possibly know that. Kate opened her mouth to say so but fatigue overwhelmed her. She was too tired to argue.

"What else did you find?" she asked instead.

Amanda took a deep breath. "I found a bunch of newspaper clippings from the 1980s. The earlier ones talked about the Gimli panty raider."

Kate's proud smile slowly faded. "Panty raider?" she interrupted. "Why were you looking for a panty raider?"

"I wasn't." Amanda shook her head to emphasize the point. "I went back to the beginning, after."

"What?" The girl wasn't making any sense.

"After I found out about Daniel Bergstrom," said Amanda. For the first time, Kate realized her niece was shaking. She took a step forward, planning to put an arm around her, but Amanda put up a hand to stop her. "I'm fine."

"All right," said Kate. "What about Daniel?" *I hope not*, Sula Olafson had said when Kate asked if Daniel was coming back. *Oh, I hope not.* "The Pettersons said he had run away with his sister."

Amanda shook her head and took another deep breath. "He's been in prison for over twenty-five years," she said. "For raping three girls."

CHAPTER 13

UNEXPECTEDLY, KATE slept very well. She woke at five-thirty, with the first glimmers of sunrise poking through her curtains, and lay staring up at the white ceiling with its weird light fixture that always reminded her of a breast.

She stretched, luxuriating in the feel of clean sheets and a well-rested body. A cool, fresh breeze wafted through the window, bringing with it the scent of freshly-mown grass and making her glad of the blankets so toasty warm around her. Then the events of the previous day came trickling back and she sighed.

She began thinking about the day ahead and the things she would have to do. Call Bert, for one. Last night, she'd found her cell phone in the pocket of the jacket she had left in the Explorer. There were three missed calls from Bert and one terse voice mail asking her to call him. By then, of course, it was midnight and too late to call. She glanced at her bedside clock. And now it was too early.

She wasn't mad at him anymore, having had time to realize that she was reacting to the tense situation between Amanda and Marco Trepalli, not Bert's words. Maybe she had subconsciously left the cell phone in the car, because she hadn't felt like talking to him. This was exactly why she avoided entanglements with other people. When you were in a relationship, you always had to negotiate, or apologize, or compromise. It was exhausting, even with someone you liked.

Even with someone you liked *a lot.*

Besides, she was no good at relationships. She always put the job first. She was old enough and wise enough now to realize it was a good thing she'd never had children. She would have been a lousy mother.

Which brought her to the next call she'd have to make. Rose. She and John would probably have some advice on what to do about Amanda. Kate's instincts urged her to slap Trepalli upside the head for hurting Amanda, but she didn't think that was a practical solution.

All comfort fled, she pushed the blankets off and sat up. Might as well face the day. It was only then that she realized she was smelling coffee. She glanced at the clock again to make sure she hadn't misread the time, then stood up. Why was Amanda up so early?

Dammit! She was going to kill that Trepalli.

She donned her slippers and a light sweatshirt over her pyjamas and shuffled down the hallway to the kitchen, where she found Amanda sitting at the kitchen counter, staring out the window, hands wrapped around a cup of coffee.

"Good morning," said Kate with determined cheerfulness.

Amanda looked around as if she hadn't heard Kate come in. "Good morning," she said, and smiled. "There's a cup left in the pot." Her blonde hair was up in a bedraggled pony tail, as if she had caught it up roughly to get it out of her face.

Kate stifled a sigh and went to the French press. She poured herself a cup, then rinsed out the glass carafe and spooned more grounds in before setting the kettle to boil.

Amanda hadn't slept. That was clear from the dark circles under her eyes and the drooping of her shoulders. Kate had to admit that a small part of her was relieved to find her niece here at all. After the sleepwalking incident, she had worried that Amanda would revert to old patterns. So, no sleepwalking, but no sleeping either. Unless...

She turned around. "You didn't sleepwalk, did you?"

Amanda smiled. "No, Aunt Kate. I told you not to worry."

Kate studied the girl's pale cheeks and bloodshot eyes. Right.

"You look like hell," she said abruptly, then could have slapped herself. Rose would not have handled it this way.

Amanda's eyebrows rose. "Don't be shy, Aunt Kate," she said earnestly, "tell me what you *really* think."

Kate grinned in spite of herself. "All right, smart ass," she grumped. "Why aren't you sleeping?"

Amanda sighed and pushed her cup away. She had on her red hoodie over her own pyjamas, but on her it looked becoming. Charming even. Kate resisted the urge to look down at herself.

"I keep thinking about Mrs. Olafson," said Amanda. "Do you suppose she knows about her son being in prison?"

Kate shrugged. "I don't know." She leaned against the counter across from Amanda and took a sip of coffee. This was a morning for honey. She reached for the jar of honey in the cupboard while considering her words. "He was incarcerated a long time ago," she said. Twenty-five years. Either there were aggravating circumstances surrounding the rapes, or he was considered a dangerous offender. Otherwise he wouldn't have served that long.

Unless, of course, he had added more crimes to his list while he was inside.

"Where did you say he was serving time?" she asked her niece as she stirred the honey into her coffee.

"The original article said Bowden Institution, in Innisfail," said Amanda. "Do you think you could check?"

Kate paused in her stirring, surprised. She had just been thinking along the same lines, but she had official reasons for wanting to check on Daniel Bergstrom's record and whereabouts, and they all had to do with the recent incidents in Mendenhall and east.

But Amanda didn't know about the underwear thefts and the break-ins.

"Why?" she finally asked.

The eyes Amanda turned on Kate were huge with fear. "I would feel better knowing he's still behind bars," she said.

Kate swallowed hard and nodded.

* * *

Bert called again just as she finished her shower. She was towelling her hair when Amanda knocked on the bathroom door. Kate wrapped the towel around herself before opening the door.

"It's Bert," said Amanda, handing Kate the mobile phone and waggling her eyebrows meaningfully. She headed for her bedroom, leaving Kate to wonder what the eyebrow thing was all about. Did she want Kate out so she could shower? The house only had one bathroom, but so far, it hadn't been a problem. Well, except that Amanda's hair, face, and body products seemed to cover every flat surface.

"Hi," she said into the phone. "Can I call you back? I'm just stepping out of the shower."

"No," said Bert grimly.

Oh. So that's what the eyebrows had meant. She figured it was a little past six. He was up very early.

She pushed the door closed again, more to keep the steamy warmth in than for privacy, and sat on the closed toilet lid. The plastic was cold against her warm flesh and she winced.

"What is it?" she said. She hoped he hadn't called just to yell at her.

"Your panty raider," he said, and Kate immediately flipped into cop mode.

"Have you found him?"

"No. But he broke into two homes last night that we know of. One's in Armstrong Point and the other one, two hours later, in East St. Paul. In the first one, he stole underwear from a fifteen-year-old girl's bedroom. He took all the underwear out and placed it around her as she slept. In East St. Paul he almost raped the girl. Her parents came home just in time, but he managed to get away."

Kate's eyes closed and her chin dropped. She should have caught him before he escalated.

"How do you know it's the same guy?" she asked softly. Winnipeg was a big city. All kinds of crimes took place there on a daily basis.

"Same M.O. And it fits the information McKell sent over."

Kate nodded. "Did he plan to rape her, do you think? Or did he grab the opportunity since she was alone?"

She could almost hear Bert's shrug. "Why don't we ask him?"

"I thought you said you didn't have him?" Kate stood up, almost vibrating with relief.

"No," said Bert quickly. "But we have his fingerprint. At least, we're pretty sure it's his fingerprint. He was careful to wipe everything down, but in his rush to get away, he missed a partial on the back door. We're running it now."

Kate stood in the rapidly cooling bathroom, her damp flesh dimpling in goose bumps, her wet hair dripping over her shoulders, staring at the closed door.

"Try Corrections Canada," she said slowly. "And check it against a Daniel Bergstrom."

There was a long silence at the other end. "Do you know something I don't?"

She shook her head automatically. "It's just a guess," she said. "But it's an educated guess."

* * *

Half an hour later, she walked into the station, letting the screen door slam shut behind her. Stan Albertson and Jim O'Hara were standing at the end of the duty counter, the log book open in front of them. They looked up in surprise as she passed by the window opening of the duty desk and strode into the duty room. O'Hara took in her uniform but didn't say a word. As usual, he was neat and clean. He glanced down at Albertson, who at five foot ten wasn't exactly short. A grey stubble covered Albertson's face and the pouches beneath his eyes were a little more pronounced than usual this morning.

"Chief." He nodded at her. "We're just going over last night's logs."

She nodded. "Go ahead. I'll listen in." She glanced at the clock above the duty desk. Quarter of seven. As if on cue, she heard a patrol car pull into the parking stall at the front of the building. At the same time, the back door opened to let Constable Holmes in.

"Ma'am," he said, nodding in greeting. His piercing blue eyes also took in her uniform. "Holiday's over?" he asked equably.

Before she could answer, the front door pushed open and Parker and Tattersall walked in.

Albertson shrugged good-naturedly. "Might as well go grab a coffee, boys," he said. "We'll wait for Gerry to get here and debrief only once."

"Where's night shift?" asked Tattersall. He was almost as tall as O'Hara's six foot three, but where O'Hara must have weighed a good two hundred and fifteen pounds, all of it muscle, Tattersall was gangly, with thinning brown hair.

"I've called Oppenheimer and Fallon back in," said Albertson, looking at Kate. "I'm keeping Boychuk and Tourmeline on patrol until day shift can relieve them."

The three new arrivals glanced at each other. Usually the shift change occurred at the station, which meant that for roughly twenty minutes every morning and twenty minutes every night, no one was patrolling. Kate caught Albertson's glance and nodded her approval. After last night's fire, she wasn't willing to leave downtown unpatrolled either.

At that moment, Oppenheimer and Fallon walked in and Kate decided to beat a strategic retreat to her office. The duty room was now officially too crowded. She'd read the log book later.

She spent the next half hour going over her email and looking up the Corrections Canada phone number. Bert was going to push through the fingerprint identification and set his staff to searching all CPIC reports about underwear thefts or assaults on young women. As deputy chief in Winnipeg, he had more people than she did. In the meantime, she wanted to find out everything she could about Daniel Bergstrom's career inside.

Eventually the noise level in the duty room died down and she emerged to find O'Hara typing away on the computer keyboard. He glanced up when she approached.

"What's happening with the fire site?" she asked.

"It's still too hot to process," he said promptly. "Firefighters dealt with a lot of hot spots overnight. Patrols reported no incidents, although I expect there'll be more activity this morning when people start arriving for work." He glanced at his screen again. "That part of the street is still blocked off. Tattersall and Abrams will be doing traffic duty during morning rush."

Kate smiled in spite of herself. The morning "rush" in Mendenhall lasted about five minutes, which long-timers found offensive. She knew of people who wouldn't wait in a line-up at the bank if there were more than three people in it. Compared to the big cities in which she had worked, Mendenhall had no traffic, and no line-ups.

It did, however, have crime.

With a sigh, she nodded her thanks. "I need you to do some research for me," she said. O'Hara didn't say anything, but his hand reached for a pen and pad of paper. A man of few words.

"Contact Corrections Canada," she continued. She handed him the yellow sticky note on which she had written the phone number. "I need you to find out about an inmate named Daniel Bergstrom. Originally from Gimli. Incarcerated about twenty-five years ago in Bowden."

"Crime?" said O'Hara without looking up.

"Sexual assault," said Kate, at which he did look up, the grooves on either side of his mouth deepening as his lips tightened. He was making connections, too. "I don't know," said Kate. "I'm just covering my bases."

"Where did the crimes take place?" asked O'Hara.

"Manitoba, I would think, but I don't know for sure," admitted Kate. "Maybe Gimli," she added after a moment, thinking of the Gimli panty raider. The Gimli panty raider could easily have escalated to rape.

He nodded and jotted more information down. "What exactly do you want to know?"

"His present location, if he's no longer in prison," said Kate. "And find out if he was ever transferred out of Bowden, and if so, why."

O'Hara nodded again and immediately picked up the phone. Kate wished Charlotte were at work today. She hated tying up the duty officer with something Charlotte could handle.

She nodded at his back and went into the lunch room to pour herself a coffee. She stood at the window overlooking the parking lot and looked at the big oak tree growing just outside. It was a cool morning, only about ten Celsius, but the forecast called for clear skies and a high of twenty-three. A glorious summer day.

And somewhere in Winnipeg, a young girl was traumatized and fearful, her family angry, all because of Daniel Bergstrom.

If it was Daniel Bergstrom.

She took a deep, tremulous breath, aware of O'Hara's low voice murmuring from the duty room. She had no proof, but the sick feeling in her gut told her she was right. She had left Amanda at home, looking like a waif in her pajamas and hoodie, and she had heard the lock click shut behind her as she walked down the few steps to the driveway. Amanda never locked the door.

Kate wished she had never heard of Gimli. Try as she might, she couldn't shake the feeling that she was missing something. The sensation was like a hair tickling her throat. Mrs. Petterson had told her Daniel and his sister had run away. Was that a lie? Or had Daniel and Sarah run away together and split up later? If so, where was Sarah now?

She needed a better timeline. She could always ask Sula Olafson when her children had run off, but she would rather talk to the Pettersons. The old man, Jakob Petterson... he was sharp. He would remember exactly when, even if Alice Petterson didn't. The dates of Daniel's crimes and his incarceration... those were a matter of public record. It was only a question of time before she found out.

A movement caught her eye in the parking lot and she watched DC McKell's Honda CRV pull in to its spot. The DC emerged from the car, his short-sleeved shirt crisply pressed, his black work shoes freshly polished, his cap under his arm. As though sensing her gaze on him, he looked unerringly at the window, even though she knew from experience that he couldn't see inside thanks to the leaves' reflection.

She watched him head for the front door, her thoughts tugging at the mystery that had somehow snared Amanda in its folds. Sula Olafson's children had been gone for nearly twenty-five years. Why was Amanda obsessed with Daniel now? Did she know something she wasn't sharing?

Kate shook her head as if to shake the idea out of her mind. No. Amanda would never keep something like that from her.

But what if Amanda had unconsciously picked up on something that Kate had missed?

The front screen door opened and McKell walked in, automatically glancing in the lunch room as he passed by. He stopped suddenly and took in her uniform. His eyebrows rose.

"So much for vacations?"

Kate shrugged and left the window to pour her coffee. She waved the pot at him and poured him a cup when he nodded. "I'm going to be here anyway," she said. "May as well make it official."

He nodded his understanding. "Anything new on the fire front?"

"No," said Kate, handing him the cup. "But there was a break-in in Winnipeg. Two, actually."

He set the cup down at the table, then sat down sideways on the chair, making sure to hitch his pant legs up a little to avoid pouching the knees.

"What happened?"

She told him about Bert's phone call and the discovery of the fingerprint. McKell's face grew harder as she filled him in.

She stopped when she became aware of another presence and they both turned toward the doorway, where O'Hara stood. His expression was grim.

"Daniel Bergstrom was sentenced to ten years in 1987 for aggravated sexual assault," he said. He looked down at the notepad in his hand. "He was incarcerated in Innisfail. One year shy of release, he killed an inmate and was sentenced to life."

Kate found she was holding her breath and forced herself to take a deep breath and relax her shoulders. McKell glanced at her but didn't say anything.

"He was released on parole a week ago Wednesday."

Kate's stomach did a slow flip.

"Location?" asked McKell.

O'Hara shrugged. "Bergstrom walked away from his halfway house on the first night and hasn't been seen since."

"Why is he here?" asked McKell. "Why come here?"

"It's where he's from," said O'Hara. "His family is in Gimli."

McKell's eyebrows rose and he turned to look at her. "Gimli."

Kate nodded. "Our cottage was next door to Sula Olafson's home, Bergstrom's mother."

McKell and O'Hara just stared at her, and finally, she shrugged. "I know it's weird, but it's a weird coincidence, nothing more."

McKell glanced at her, clearly suspecting there was more to it, but all he said was, "Edmonton's seven hundred and fifty miles from here. I doubt he'd have taken a bus, or bought a car. He either stole one or hitchhiked."

"Why didn't Edmonton report him missing?" asked Kate. None of the CPIC reports had mentioned Bergstrom and she'd seen no

Be On the Look Out alerts, or BOLOs, for him.

"Don't know," said O'Hara, as the phone started ringing. He edged toward the duty room, still talking over his shoulder. "Near as I can figure out, someone screwed up." He hurried out to answer the phone.

She wondered if the Gimli detachment knew. That was always the first place you looked for a fugitive—the place they had come from. Depending on his luck with hitchhiking, he could have been in Mendenhall last Saturday. When the first theft of underwear was reported.

McKell was clearly thinking along the same lines she was. "We checked the communities west of here," he said. "No reports of underwear theft, no assaults. Why would he have started in Mendenhall?"

Kate shrugged. How the heck was she supposed to know? She was a cop, not a psychologist.

"Maybe at first he was too busy running," she guessed. "Maybe by the time he reached Mendenhall, he was feeling more secure. Or maybe more anxious. He was getting close to home."

"Or maybe, now that he's free, he has trouble controlling the compulsion." McKell shook his head in frustration.

Kate nodded, aware that they were committing a cardinal sin in police work. Assuming. They were assuming that Bergstrom was heading for Gimli. Her gut was telling her it was a safe assumption but it wasn't logical. Why head for home? He surely didn't expect his elderly mother to welcome him home. Did he have a nest egg hidden away somewhere? Enough money to help him hide? Did he think his mother had money?

Or did he think his sister would be there? She felt cold suddenly and rubbed her arms.

"I don't know, Rob," she said. "But I have a bad feeling."

McKell nodded. "Yeah. So do I."

CHAPTER 14

IT WAS mid-afternoon before Bert called with the fingerprint identification.

"It's him," he said. "We've notified the Gimli detachment, but you know as well as I do that they don't have the staff to handle this."

Kate nodded, even though he couldn't see her at the other end of the line. "I know." She took a deep breath and leaned forward, resting her elbows on her desk. "I'm going back."

"Whoa," said Bert immediately. "What for? You're in no better position to find this guy than the locals are. I've sent a couple of my guys down to help out."

Good. That would help. But every time she started to relax, she saw an image of Sula Olafson's stricken face when Kate announced that she and Amanda had to go. The thought of that old woman all alone when her son returned...

"Kate?"

"Still here," she said. "I need to check something out. Call you later." She hung up before he could say anything and she silently promised she would make all this up to him. Somehow.

She popped her head out her office. Sunlight streamed through the open back door, as did the warm breeze. O'Hara looked up from the bank of filing cabinets behind Charlotte's desk.

"When is Charlotte back?" she asked him.

"Tomorrow," he said. "Did you need something?"

She shook her head. "I can handle it."

She headed back to her office and sat down in front of the computer. Amanda had said she had found the information on genealogy sites and she'd mentioned archived newspaper files. Kate suddenly dredged a word out of her memory banks. Back in the day, newspapers used to keep their old copies in a room called the morgue.

She shied away from the sudden image and opened a search engine. It took half an hour, but she finally found what she was looking for.

* * *

She was on the phone with the Fire Chief Jon Avramson, getting an update on the fire, when Trepalli burst into her office.

"I'll have to call you back, Chief," she said calmly as Trepalli stood looking at her. His eyes were wide and his nostrils flared. She couldn't tell if he was scared or mad.

"What's the problem, Constable?" she asked coolly.

He wore a short-sleeved polo shirt that was caught in the belt of his jeans in the back. His hair was dishevelled, as if he'd been clutching at it, and he clearly hadn't shaved today. She had never seen him look so rumpled.

"Chief, it's Amanda," he said in a low voice. Behind him, Kate saw O'Hara hovering with a frown and she shook her head at him minutely. It was time for her to deal with Marco Trepalli.

"She's gone," he added when Kate didn't respond.

Kate shrugged. "What do you mean by 'gone'?"

"She's not at home," he said at once. "We were going to meet there and talk."

Kate hated the idea of Trepalli bringing his fight with Amanda to the house, but that wasn't her main concern right now.

"I know what you're going to say," said Trepalli, pre-empting her. He walked into the office and over to the window, clearly unaware of the breach of protocol. Or uncaring. She should have tried harder to nip this in the bud.

"But she finally agreed to talk to me," he said, turning around to face her. "She's the one who called me."

Okay, that was a little weird. Why would she have called him over only to leave before he showed up?

"Did you wait?" she asked reasonably. "She might have gone to run an errand."

"She wouldn't," said Trepalli with the quiet certainty of a man who never doubted himself. Kate almost rolled her eyes.

"Constable, she probably doesn't want to talk to you," she said sharply. "You must have misunderstood her."

He turned haunted eyes to her. "Something is wrong," he said.

She waited but he didn't add anything and much as she wanted to, she couldn't argue with his assessment.

Something was definitely wrong.

"Did anything happen in Gimli?" he asked finally.

A shiver ran up her scalp and she shook off the sudden feeling of someone walking over her grave.

"What do you mean?" she asked.

"She... I don't know. She mentioned Gimli when I talked to her this morning."

Kate swallowed to ease her suddenly dry throat. Gimli was beginning to loom in her life like some monster gaining on her.

"Why did you guys cut your trip short?" continued Trepalli. "Did something happen?"

Damn it. "No, nothing happened," she said impatiently. "We were having trouble sleeping. She sleepwalked one night. We just wanted to be home."

He turned to face her fully and his blue, blue eyes sharpened to laser-like intensity. She became aware of the sounds of constables in the duty room and the smell of coffee wafting in. Someone had made a fresh pot. But try as she might, she couldn't tear her gaze from Trepalli's.

"Why was she having trouble sleeping?"

"She." Not "you." Kate almost smiled.

"The neighbor was a little noisy at night," she said simply.

Trepalli stared at her, clearly aware that she wasn't telling him the whole story but unsure of how to proceed.

The sound of footsteps approached and they both looked around to see McKell in the doorway.

"We may have caught the arsonist."

* * *

"Caught" was perhaps a strong word. Someone had reported seeing a stranger buying containers of gasoline at the PetroCan. They had noted the make and color of the car—a '92 baby blue Impala—and the license plate number. It was an Alberta plate.

"We ran it," said McKell. "It belongs to a Minnie Stratford, an eighty-year-old who lives in Airdrie."

"Reported stolen?" asked Kate.

McKell shook his head. His gaze flickered over to Trepalli, who was still standing by the window, but he didn't ask. "Mrs. Stratford is legally blind but she has a nephew, Lucas Tormegev. Tormegev spent the last ten years in Bowden for arson. He was released three months ago. According to the Parole Board, he's been living in Edmonton."

"Does he have any family in Mendenhall?" asked Kate. Why would Tormegev have driven all the way from Edmonton via Airdrie to start torching her town?

McKell shook his head. "Airdrie police are interviewing Mrs. Stratford, but so far we've uncovered no connection."

"Do we know where Mr. Tormegev is now?" asked Kate.

"Motel just outside of town. I've got Holmes and Parker watching the place."

Kate stood up. "Good work. Let's invite Mr. Tormegev in for questioning."

McKell nodded. "He blew off his parole officer in Edmonton, so we can hold him until Edmonton police come fetch him."

"Does he know the panty raider?" asked Trepalli, startling Kate and McKell.

Kate opened her mouth then closed it. Was that it? Was that the connection?

"That's a good question, Constable," she said slowly. "Why don't you call the correction facility in Innisfail and ask the warden if Tormegev and Bergstrom know each other."

Even though he was off duty, Trepalli nodded and pushed away from the window. He edged past the DC and headed for one of the empty desks in the duty room. McKell left, too, to order Holmes and Parker to bring Tormegev in, leaving Kate alone in her office.

Her gaze found the window and the blue sky beyond. Where was Amanda? Impulsively, she picked up her telephone and dialed Amanda's cell phone, only to hang up when she reached the girl's voice mail.

An image of Mrs. Olafson popped into her mind, and she frowned. She picked up the phone again and this time, dialed the land line at the house. After six rings, she hung up.

She called Bert. "Any news on Daniel Bergstrom?" she asked when he picked up.

"Not yet," said Bert, not missing a beat. He was used to her peremptory manner. "What's going on?"

Kate shrugged, even though he couldn't see her. "I don't know yet," she said. "We may have found our arsonist."

"Good," said Bert. "It's bad enough you sent us your rapist— we don't want your arsonist, too."

Kate knew he was teasing, but it touched on her guilt at not stopping Daniel sooner.

Not that he was stopped.

She sighed and Bert's voice lowered. "What's going on, Katie?" he asked. His voice was like a caress and she felt absurdly grateful that he was there for her to talk to.

"I don't know," she said truthfully. "I can't put my finger on it."

"You will," he said confidently. "You'll figure it out."

They hung up and Kate sat back in her chair, trying to under-stand why her stomach was in knots. She had missed something.

* * *

Ten minutes later, O'Hara popped his head into her office.

"Holmes and Parker brought Tormegev in. DC McKell is getting ready to question him."

Kate nodded and stood up. They had agreed to let McKell interrogate Tormegev first. The DC could be intimidating when he wanted to.

She walked into the duty room to find Kyle Holmes with a bloody nose and Colin Parker with a torn shirt pocket.

"What happened?"

"Little bastard just about got away from us," said Holmes. He sat at Charlotte's desk and held a wad of tissues against his nose with a big hand. His short blond hair looked spikier than ever, but maybe that was the result of the tussle.

Parker didn't look up from the log book where he was making an entry, but his slash of a mouth quirked into a smile. At six foot four, he was easily the biggest constable on the force, but Kate had never heard him swear or seen him get mad.

"DC's got him in the interview room," he said.

"Where did Trepalli go?" asked Kate, looking around.

At the duty desk, O'Hara looked around. "He's watching the interview."

Kate nodded and left the duty room, heading for the identifica-tion room. She wanted to watch the interview, too.

The interview room was tucked at the back of the ident room, where fingerprints were taken and old files were kept. Essentially, someone years ago had put a wall up at the end of the ident room and put a door and a one-sided window in the wall.

Anyone who had ever watched a cop show would know about the one-sided window, but it was a matter of convention that the light in the interview room was only turned on after the interviewee had entered. No need to rub in the fact that he would be on display.

A small man sat at the table facing the window, dressed in a clean white shirt with the sleeves rolled up to reveal corded arms. A small control panel was embedded in the table top. It controlled the recording equipment. Kate hoped McKell had informed Tormegev that he was being recorded.

Tormegev's hair was short and full. It could have been sandy, or brown with a lot of gray. It was hard to tell in the uncertain light of the interview room. His wrists rested on the table top, his fingers linked as if he were a child praying.

He looked like a high school teacher.

McKell was in the room, too, standing nonchalantly to one side of the table, ignoring the witness while he read through a file.

Trepalli stood in front of the one-way glass, his legs apart, his arms crossed. He looked around when she arrived.

"We've already got a file on him?" she asked.

He grinned humorlessly. "No. O'Hara is getting it now from Bowden Correctional Institute. From what Holmes and Parker told me, the guy's not talking. I think the DC's trying to sweat him."

Kate looked at the man sitting patiently inside the interview room. He did not look like a man who had bloodied the nose of one constable and ripped the shirt of another. According to DC McKell, Tormegev had done ten years for arson. It would probably take more than McKell silently reading a file to "sweat" him.

"What did you find out?" she asked Trepalli.

He kept his gaze on the man in the chair. "They know each other," he said grimly. "Tormegev and Bergstrom shared a cell for six years in Innisfail."

And there was her connection. Prison could destroy the humanity of men, but it could also form strong bonds. Was this what had happened here?

"Does DC McKell know?" she asked.

Trepalli nodded.

Holmes and Parker wandered in and stood quietly behind her and Trepalli. The viewing "gallery" was small. Holmes had cleaned the blood from his face, but a white tissue stuck out from one nostril. Kate tried not to stare.

O'Hara, still stuck on the duty desk, would be able to view the interview on the computer—one of the few technical improvements she'd been able to bring to the detachment.

Mayor and council refused to allot more money to add computers to the patrol cars, let alone spring for more personnel, but this they had allowed her: one small camera installed in the interview room and connected to the detachment's computer system.

Everybody preferred watching the interview unroll in front of them, of course.

She made a mental note to ask O'Hara to follow up on the video clip they had sent to Brandon for analysis. She glanced at her watch. It was only three-thirty. It was probably too early to expect anything.

"Mr. Tormegev," said McKell suddenly, his voice coming through the speaker in the wall. "You are far from home."

Lucas Tormegev looked at McKell but said nothing. His eyes were a dark chocolate brown.

"In fact," continued McKell, "you aren't supposed to be anywhere near Manitoba at all." He looked at the man. "What brings you here?"

Tormegev shrugged. "The air is better."

McKell nodded solemnly. "This is true. Or at least, it was true until a few days ago. There's been a lot of smoke in the air lately."

Tormegev smiled.

McKell closed the file and dropped it on the table before sitting down. "Do you have family here?"

Tormegev shrugged. "You've read my file. You tell me."

McKell grinned tightly. "No family. So, it must be something else—or maybe someone else—that brings you here."

Tormegev remained silent and Kate had to tamp down a spike of impatience. This was why McKell was better at interviewing. He could outwait almost anybody.

The ident room was starting to feel a little claustrophobic and Kate controlled an urge to get Parker to step back. He was crowding her, but the quarters were tight. Still, when his breath ruffled the hair on top of her head, she gave him a look and he took a step back.

"Lucas, where were you last night, say between six p.m. and seven p.m.?"

Tormegev just looked at McKell. "I've done my time, screw. I'm free and clear. Don't need to tell you a damned thing."

McKell looked genuinely surprised. "That's not what your parole officer's been telling me," he said. "In fact, he said you missed your last few appointments with him." He tapped the closed file with his index finger. "My guess is that's because you were on your way here with Daniel Bergstrom."

Tormegev's start of surprise was slight but they all saw it. Almost as one, they leaned in as if to hear better, but McKell acted as if he hadn't noticed anything.

"Did you drive? Or did you hitchhike?" He shook his head. "No one would pick up two men hitchhiking. You drove. You were out three months ahead of Daniel, plenty of time to find yourself some wheels."

He flipped open the file again, making sure to keep the contents out of Tormegev's sight. "But you didn't have to look far, did you?" he said, glancing from the file folder to Tormegev's face. "It says here that car you were driving belongs to your aunt Minnie. She didn't even know it was gone. Heck, Lucas," he added reproachfully, "she didn't even know you were out of jail."

Even in the uncertain light of the interview room, there was no disguising the tide of red that crept over Tormegev's neck and face. Kate almost smiled. That was the chink in Tormegev's armor.

McKell nodded as if Tormegev had just confirmed something for him.

"So here's how I see it, Lucas." McKell closed the file and leaned forward on his elbows, using the index finger of his right hand to tick off the points on the fingers of his left hand. "You're on parole but you missed your last three appointments with your parole officer. That alone will haul you back in front of the Parole Board. Two: you are suspected of associating with a known felon, Daniel Bergstrom. Also a big no-no, as far as the board is concerned. And last but not least, we suspect you of setting a number of fires in our community." His hands suddenly slapped down on the table, startling Kate and the others and making Tormegev jump.

"And that, Lucas," he said softly, "means I get to keep you while we investigate."

Tormegev's expression grew truculent. "You've got nothing on me," he said. "Unless you planted evidence."

McKell laughed out loud. He leaned forward, his muscled forearms stretched out on the table top. "We don't need to plant evidence, Lucas," he assured the man. "We just need to gather it."

* * *

Kate and McKell stood side by side, looking over O'Hara's shoulder as he scrolled through Tormegev's prison file.

"There!" said McKell suddenly, clamping a hand on O'Hara's shoulder and making the poor man jump.

"What?" said Kate, staring at the words, waiting for whatever he'd seen to jump out at her.

"Go back up," ordered McKell and O'Hara obediently scrolled up. "There," said McKell again, this time pointing to a spot on the screen. Kate studied it. It was the box reserved for notes by the warden of Bowden. In this one, the warden had indicated that Bergstrom and Tormegev had become cell mates after Bergstrom's cell mate was released. There was a terse note that the two seemed to have formed a bond and the warden suspected it might be sexual. Either way, it resulted in fewer altercations between Bergstrom and the other inmates and a reduction in the number of suspicious small fires that had been plaguing the institution for the past few months.

"Cell mates," said Kate, straightening up.

"*Close* cell mates," said McKell, looking down at her.

"He was released in March," O'Hara pointed out. He turned in his stool to look at both of them and his knees brushed against McKell's legs. Kate stepped off the small platform, quickly followed by McKell. Not ten minutes ago she had been irritated at Parker for crowding her in front of the one-way glass, and here she was doing the same thing to poor O'Hara.

He smiled his thanks and continued. "But Bergstrom was only released a week ago."

"About the time Tormegev stopped checking in with his parole officer," said McKell.

Kate nodded. It fit. "They were lovers. What else do we know about Tormegev?"

"Umm..." O'Hara scrolled through the pages until he got to the visitor section. "Looks like he only ever got one visitor, his aunt." He stopped and peered at the picture on the screen.

"What is it?" asked McKell, crowding closer.

Kate almost sighed. The two sets of wide male shoulders effectively blocked her view of the screen.

As if choreographed, O'Hara and McKell both pulled back and turned their heads at the same time to look over their shoulders at her.

"What?" said Kate, nonplussed.

"She kinda looks like you," said O'Hara.

"Who?" asked Kate.

"Aunt Minnie," said McKell. He stepped back to allow her access to the computer and she peered at the picture on the screen.

It was an old woman. Like, really old. Kate's left eyebrow rose and she turned to look at her deputy chief.

He blushed. "Look past the age difference," he said gruffly.

Next to her, O'Hara's shoulders moved suspiciously but she refused to look at him. Kate spent a moment studying Minnie Stratford's photo.

Well, all right. The woman looked to be in her mid-seventies but once she got past that, Kate had to admit that there was a certain cursory resemblance. Minnie Stratford had a round face and blue eyes, and she kept her white hair in a bun at the back of her neck. Her bangs were thick and well-trimmed and she seemed to be wearing a flowery cotton shirt buttoned to her neck, beneath a royal blue cardigan that only had the top button fastened. A pair of glasses hung from a cord around her neck.

Minnie Stratford looked like everybody's favorite grandmother.

Besides the round face and blue eyes, there was no resemblance. Kate didn't have a motherly bone in her body.

"Okay," said McKell. "We've let him stew long enough. I'm going back in."

Kate put a hand out to stop him. "Wait," she said slowly. She looked around at him. "I'll do it."

McKell might be the better interviewer, but he was a big, military-looking guy where Kate was small and round and apparently she would remind Tormegev of his grandmother.

McKell looked doubtful but Kate strode from the duty room and into the ident room. Trepalli was the only one left watching Tormegev. He turned at her approach.

"Any word from Amanda?" he asked hopefully.

Kate shook her head. No word. She was beginning to share the boy's concern. Where the hell was she? But Amanda was a grown woman. She didn't have to tell Kate where she was going. And right now, Kate had to worry about this potential arsonist.

Still, why didn't Amanda answer her cell phone?

Tormegev looked up as she entered the interview room, and she suspected that he had been napping. Or pretending to nap.

"Mr. Tormegev," she said politely. "My name is Kate Williams. I'm the chief of police in Mendenhall."

She waited for him to acknowledge her with a nod before pulling out the chair in front of him and sitting down. She caught a faint whiff of sour sweat and hoped it was coming from him and not her. She pulled the chair in and settled herself comfortably, her hands resting on top of each other on the table top.

Tormegev was fifteen years younger than her, but there was a defiance in him that seemed almost adolescent.

He stared back at her, studying her as she studied him. Finally she sighed.

"You're in trouble, Lucas," she said softly, keeping her expression gentle. "But you can still come out of this with a life."

Whatever he had been expecting, it wasn't sympathy. "What do you mean?" he asked cautiously.

"You've served your time," she said. Her hands rose and parted to indicate the room around them. "Haven't you had enough of places like this?" She allowed herself a small smile. "Aren't you ready to put all this behind you? You're still a young man. You have people who care about you. Your Aunt Minnie visited you every week until her eyesight got too bad to drive safely."

His gaze dropped to the table top and he swallowed hard. Kate rested her hands back on the table, close to his but not touching.

"It wasn't your idea to come here, was it, Lucas?"

He glanced at her, then dropped his gaze again, but she had seen a glimpse of uncertainty in his eyes.

"It was his idea, wasn't it?" She held her breath as his hands clenched into fists. The smell of sour sweat grew stronger. Definitely not her.

"Daniel's the one who convinced you to take Aunt Minnie's car, didn't he?" she continued softly. Her right hand rose as if to touch his clenched fist, then she let it drop back to the table. "You would never have abused your aunt's trust like that, if not for him."

She almost whispered the last, watching the top of Tormegev's brown hair. She caught a minute shake of his head and, suddenly inspired, kept going. "And now, after turning you into a fugitive, where is he? Daniel's left you all alone, hasn't he?"

A tear drop rolled down Tormegev's cheek and dropped to the table top. Kate's hand found his fist. She patted it gently and he looked up at her.

"Isn't that what happened?" she asked softly.

"He just left me here," he said, a catch in his voice. His eyes were brown and bloodshot and there was no disguising the pain in them. "I told him I wanted him to stop it with stealing underwear, that he'd get caught, but..." He shook his head. "It was like he couldn't hear me," he added, tears welling up in his eyes again. "He was... different. Strange. Scary," he added with a whisper. He took a deep breath. "We didn't even fight. He just walked out the door of the motel and didn't come back."

Kate nodded her understanding. "He took your aunt's car. Where was he going?"

Lucas hesitated. He shot her a glance then turned away.

Kate waited ten seconds to be sure he wasn't going to answer. "Lucas?" she said softly. "He was going to Gimli, wasn't he?"

Tormegev blew out a sigh that left him looking smaller. Deflated. He nodded. "I'm pretty sure," he said. "He kept talking about going home, seeing his mother and his sister."

His sister? Kate tried to control the sudden spike of interest. She didn't want to spook him. But she had to know.

"Why does he think his sister will be there?" she asked.

Lucas looked up at her, clearly confused by her question. "That must be where she lives," he said.

Kate desperately wanted to look over her shoulder at the one-way glass, but she kept her attention on Tormegev.

"You don't need to hide anymore," she said. "It's time to go back to Edmonton and get your life back. Aunt Minnie will be waiting for you." She injected a note of sternness in her voice. "But first, I want you to tell me why you lit those fires. I can still help you with your parole officer, but I need to know why you set those fires in my town."

And now she held her breath because they were venturing onto different territory, his territory. He was a fire bug and had already served time for arson. He had to know that admitting to the Mendenhall fires would land him back in jail.

His gaze remained level and she saw awareness in his eyes. For a few moments they remained like that, gazes locked, in silent communication. Finally he shrugged and broke eye contact.

"The fires make me feel better," he said quietly. "I don't hurt people. I just like to see things burn."

Kate nodded. Yes. She didn't understand the compulsion to burn things, but she did understand the need to do something—anything—to take the pain and loneliness away.

She sighed softly. "All right, Lucas. I'll get a pad of paper and a pen, and you can write out your statement."

He sighed, too, and it sounded almost like a sigh of relief.

CHAPTER 15

AMANDA STILL wasn't answering the phone, either the land line at the house or her cell phone. Kate put down the receiver and stifled an urge to get in the Explorer and go check on her. Trepalli had already checked the house twice since she had finished her interview with Tormegev. The girl wasn't home.

Kate leaned back in her desk chair and stared out the window. The sun was on its downward sweep, lengthening shadows in the parking lot even though there were still at least four hours of daylight left. Dinnertime. In the duty room, she could make out O'Hara talking to someone on the phone. She thought she'd heard Tattersall come in earlier. He was probably in the lunch room, eating. Tormegev was in a cell. Edmonton officers would be arriving tomorrow to take him back. She hoped O'Hara would remember to arrange dinner for the man.

She's a grown woman. She can go where she likes, when she likes. And you've got a rapist to find.

But, like Trepalli, Kate had a bad feeling. It just wasn't like Amanda to leave without letting Kate know where she was going and when she'd be back.

She kept thinking back to their conversation in the parking lot last night. She thought about Amanda's sympathy for Sula

Olafson. About how the older woman's hand had kept reaching out to touch Amanda, as if to make sure she was really there. How a woman wept every night at one-fifteen.

How Daniel Bergstrom seemed to be heading for Gimli...

She took a deep breath and glanced at her computer screen, at the photograph of Sula Olafson and her husband, Malcolm Bergstrom, along with their children. It had been published in the *Gimli Weekly* in 1985, the summer Daniel and Sarah disappeared. It had been taken a few years earlier, when the kids were fifteen and sixteen. By the decorated tree in the corner, it was obviously a Christmas photograph, the kind that went into newsletters that were popular at the time.

The photograph was grainy, and if she tried to enlarge it too much it became pixilated, but even so, there was some resemblance between Sarah Bergstrom and Amanda. Both were tall and slim, with long hair and oval faces, and wide, welcoming smiles. But that was a superficial resemblance at best. Sarah had dark hair, unlike her brother's blond, blond hair. It was hard to tell if the resemblance went beyond that. Kate could have kicked herself for not paying more attention when she was in Sula Olafson's house. Had there been photographs there?

It didn't matter. Sula would have given the newspaper the best photograph possible of her kids.

The door to her office pushed open and Trepalli stood in the doorway. His face looked thin and there were lines on either side of his mouth. She looked her question at him and he shook his head. Still no sign of her.

Kate took a deep breath.

"All right, Constable," she said softly. "Let's go to Gimli."

* * *

She had expected Bert to try and talk her out of it, but he surprised her.

"I'll wait for you at the viewing area by the big burn."

Trepalli was driving her Explorer, leaving her free to talk on the cell phone. She had changed into the civvies she kept at the office. She had no official business in Gimli and it would be offensive to show up in uniform. Trepalli was already in his civvies.

She hadn't told McKell where they were going, but he had seen her leave with Trepalli. She had no doubt that he would figure it out.

"You don't have to come," she said, more out of obligation than out of conviction. The truth was, she missed Bert—missed his calm, his solidity, his humor. She hadn't seen him in ten days and phone calls just weren't cutting it any more.

"Just try to keep me away," he said and then signed off. With a sigh, she punched in the number for the duty desk.

"Mendenhall Police," said O'Hara after the first ring.

"It's me," said Kate. "Any sign of the aunt's car?"

"None."

"Any reports of stolen cars?"

"No, ma'am," he replied. "Nothing for almost three weeks. He could have taken the bus," he added doubtfully.

Kate shook her head. "There's a BOLO out on the guy." Better late than never. "All the bus companies between Toronto and Edmonton have a copy of his photo. Keep me posted."

"Yes, ma'am," he said and hung up.

No reports of stolen cars, and likely no bus. He wouldn't dare hitchhike, would he?

Would he be stupid enough to be driving Tormegev's aunt's car?

Kate slipped the phone back in her jacket pocket, stuffed between the two seats. There was a BOLO out on the car, too. They'd find him.

She had changed into her favorite jeans and a white, short-sleeved camp shirt, and a pair of running shoes. A little warm, maybe, but at least she'd be ready for anything.

She glanced at Trepalli but he was focused on the road ahead. He had settled on exactly the speed limit after she had spoken to him sharply, and now he drove with both hands clenched on the steering wheel, leaning forward slightly as if willing the Explorer to get there faster.

"Would you like me to drive?" she asked.

"No."

Her eyebrows rose at his sharp reply but she didn't say anything. They were both on edge. No sense getting into a fight.

This was her favorite time of day, when the shadows lengthened, making the fields look soft as velvet. Normally the drive to Winnipeg relaxed her. It was something about the big sky and the far horizon—it always made her feel as if she could breathe deeply here. But today was different. Today her hands clutched the shoulder belt and her jaw was clenched so tightly she was getting a headache.

They were already approaching the outskirts of Winnipeg and the traffic was growing heavier. She could almost feel the waves of frustration coming off Trepalli.

They encountered more traffic as they got closer, but most of it was heading into Winnipeg proper, while they were bypassing the city. Within twenty minutes, they had passed by the city and were rolling at the speed limit again. Kate kept an eye on the mile markers and was about to tap Trepalli on the arm when he began to slow down to take the turn-off into the viewing area where Bert was going to meet them.

The viewing area was nothing more than a pull-out with parking for a dozen vehicles—empty now except for the Explorer—and a couple of outhouses. It overlooked a vast swamp that sloped away from the highway toward a forest half a kilometer away. The swamp was dotted with burned matchstick trees that poked out of murky water like black ghosts still tethered to hell.

An interpretive sign gave some of the natural history of the place, including the fact that a forest fire had raged through the area in 1979, changing the ecosystem and chasing the forest dwellers out. Kate couldn't imagine anyone feeling better after reading it and looking out at that landscape. The place gave her the creeps.

She and Trepalli stayed in the Explorer, their backs to the swamp. A moment later, Bert drove up in his green Honda CRV and she got out to greet him. He pulled the hand brake on and jumped out of the CRV to give her a big bear hug. She hugged him back fiercely, not even caring that Trepalli could see. At least he'd stayed in the car.

Bert pulled back but kept his hands on her shoulders. He wore his summer dress uniform, without the jacket, and the short sleeves revealed his muscled, freckled, sunburned arms with the golden red hair glistening in the sun. She loved that he was only a few inches taller than her five foot three. It always felt like she could see directly into his soul. His copper-penny eyes crinkled in a smile as he looked at her.

"When's the last time you tried calling her?" he asked.

Kate shrugged. "About half an hour ago."

"Have you asked the patrols to keep an eye out for her?"

Kate opened her mouth, then closed it. She hadn't. It hadn't even occurred to her. Patrols were her work life. Amanda was her home life. She'd been working very hard at keeping the two separate, especially after Amanda and Trepalli started dating. She sighed and shook her head.

"It's not abusing your power," said Bert firmly, completely mis-understanding her. "They'll just keep an eye out and let you know if they see her. It's reassurance."

"The DC has already asked patrols to keep an eye open," came Trepalli's voice from the Explorer.

They both turned to face him and he lowered the window all the way. He didn't even try to pretend he hadn't been eavesdropping. It struck her suddenly how much older he looked than he had even a few weeks ago.

"They all know her car," he continued. "They'll let me know if they spot her in Mendenhall."

That felt almost like collaborative stalking and Kate didn't care.

It was a relief to know there would be many pairs of eyes watching for Amanda.

"When did you ask...?"

Trepalli shook his head and leaned his elbow on the door's edge, the better to lean out. "I didn't ask. DC McKell did. Two hours ago."

The words hit her like a punch in the gut. In two hours, none of the patrols had sighted Amanda's car. She pulled away from Bert.

"Let's go," she said.

"Hang on," said Bert, grabbing for her hand. "I want to show you where the perimeter is." He dragged her to his Honda, as if afraid she would take off if he let go of her. "Trepalli, you'll need to see this, too," he called over his shoulder.

Behind her, the door to the Explorer opened and a moment later, Trepalli stood by her side. They both waited while Bert fished through his glove box and emerged with a map, which he laid flat on the hood of the CRV.

It was a topographical map of Gimli. Kate leaned in and with her finger, traced the outline of the lakeshore, past the town site, to Stony Point, where the Olafson cottage stood.

"There," she said, her finger poised on the point of land. "That's where the two cottages are."

Bert nodded. He pulled the stub of a pencil out of his uniform shirt pocket and drew a cross on Fireweed Road. "The Gimli detachment has set up a watcher right here," he said.

Technically, that would be enough. After all, Fireweed Road was the only way to the point. And the road ended beyond Mrs. Olafson's house.

Kate considered what she knew of the point. "Do we know for sure that he isn't already there?" she asked slowly. The thought chilled her. Mrs. Olafson would not welcome her son back, especially if he had escaped from his halfway house and believed that his sister would be waiting for him back home. Was that why the woman had seemed dismayed at the thought he would come back? Had she lied to him?

But the penal records showed not one visit to Daniel Bergstrom in all the years he had been incarcerated. Not one.

"Hard to know for sure," admitted Bert. "Gimli Detachment's been watching the place, but the only person they've seen is the old woman."

Kate nodded, although she was far from reassured.

"She has a telephone," she said, suddenly remembering. "She must have." Jakob Petterson had mentioned that she called for groceries, and called them when she had a problem with the house. "Has anyone tried calling her?"

"I don't know, Katie," said Bert. "We can get all the details when we get there."

"What about water access?" asked Trepalli. "How hard would it be to boat over from Gimli?"

Bert glanced at the constable and sighed. "In a motorboat, maybe twenty minutes. But he'd have to go through Gimli, get to the marina, and steal a boat. That's a lot riskier than overland."

Trepalli nodded but his lips were pressed tightly together.

"Let's go," said Kate abruptly. She hated this helplessness. Hated knowing she wasn't in charge of protecting that old lady. Hated knowing that somehow, Amanda was involved in this situation. She needed to get to the point and see for herself that Amanda wasn't there.

"Want to ride with me?" asked Bert. His hand stroked her bare arm. She shook her head. She didn't dare leave Trepalli to drive alone. "All right," said Bert equably. "You lead. It's been years since I've been down there."

Both she and Trepalli nodded and turned toward the Explorer. A wind had sprung up and Kate looked up to see clouds beginning to pile up on the horizon. Lake Winnipeg could be dangerous in a storm, she suddenly remembered.

With any luck, they would be at the point long before the

storm—if there was going to be one—broke. Maybe Mrs. Olafson could go to the Pettersons until her son was apprehended.

"Bert," she called as a thought suddenly struck her. He paused with his hand on the open driver's door and looked at her. In the long shadows, his eyes looked almost black. Trepalli stopped and turned around, too.

"What about the cottage next door?" she asked. "The one we rented? Did anyone check it?"

Bert shook his head to indicate his lack of knowledge.

"Can you find out if there's a car parked there?" she insisted.

Bert opened his mouth to say something, then paused. What he saw on her face clearly made him reconsider. "I'll ask," he said gently.

"Call me," she said.

And with that, they climbed back into their respective vehicles and headed back onto the highway. Fifteen minutes later, Bert called to inform her that there were no cars parked in front of the rental cottage.

It was another forty-five minutes before they reached Gimli, and another five minutes before they pulled into the parking lot of the Gimli detachment of the RCMP.

A civilian woman sat at the duty desk behind bullet-proof glass. A wall behind her blocked the view to offices and duty room, but Kate could hear male and female voices and as they approached, a woman in a Portage Police Department uniform walked behind the duty desk, talking on a cell phone.

"Deputy Chief Bert Langdon, Winnipeg Police Services," said Bert into the speaker mounted in the glass. He pulled out his iden-tification and showed it. "This is Chief Williams, Mendenhall, and Constable Trepalli, also Mendenhall."

"Thank you, Chief," said the woman. "Your people are in the incident room." She pointed to her left. "I'll buzz you in." She was in her mid-forties, with a no-nonsense, competent air about her, but Kate couldn't help but notice the woman giving Trepalli the once over. *Brother.*

Kate nodded her thanks and followed Bert through the door, Trepalli close on her heels. Was a locked door truly necessary? In *Gimli*? But the RCMP were high profile and easily targeted, especially in small communities. It probably made sense to have as many safeguards in place as feasible.

The door opened onto the hallway, and immediately to the right, the hallway opened up into a big room twice the size of her own duty room, with a number of desks and privacy partitions. The overhead lights were on to counter the growing darkness outside the windows. A big table had been set up in the middle of the room with half-a-dozen chairs around it, laptops, and maps. The Portage officer was still on her cell phone, but tracing a finger on the map. Across from her, two Winnipeg Police Services officers worked on their laptops, leaning over to look at each other's screens and feeding information to the woman on the phone. They all looked up and stopped talking as Kate, Bert, and Trepalli walked in. The two Winnipeg officers scrambled to their feet and stood at attention.

"Sir!" they said in unison.

Kate raised a sardonic eyebrow at Bert, who shrugged slightly.

"As you were," he said. "Report."

Kate couldn't help the small thrill she felt every time she saw evidence of Bert's authority. He was such a laid-back guy that she often forgot he was the second-in-charge of a major metropolitan police force.

The Portage officer nodded politely but resumed her conversation on the cell phone. The younger Winnipeg constable returned to his seat while the older one approached so he wouldn't have to raise his voice. His name tag read SCHOFIELD. He had dark hair and eyes, and Kate figured him for his mid-thirties. He might have been First Nation, or at least have some First Nation in him.

"No sign of him," said Schofield. "Gimli detachment has two officers watching the house. No roadblocks, as per orders." He glanced at Kate and Trepalli, clearly unsure of the reason for their presence and uncertain as to how much he should be saying. Before Kate could do more than glance at Bert, he spoke up.

"This is Chief Williams, Mendenhall, and Constable Trepalli," said Bert. He was much shorter than Schofield but there was no doubt as to who was in charge. "She's rented the cottage next door to the Olafson house. She and I plan to set up there and provide coverage from that location."

Kate controlled her start of surprise. She had been planning exactly that but hadn't spoken to him about it. Frankly, she had expected resistance.

"Sir," said Trepalli, stepping closer. He was about to object to being left out but Kate shook her head.

"If she's here," she said softly, "her car will be, too. You need to look for it."

"She, who?" asked Schofield, confused.

"My niece," said Kate.

At that moment, an RCMP officer walked in from one of the back offices. He took in their presence and nodded politely. Clearly the woman on the duty desk had called him.

"Staff Sergeant Giles Corcoran," he said.

Bert introduced them and Corcoran nodded to Kate and Trepalli in turn. At a nod from Bert, Schofield returned to the table and Bert explained to the officer what they planned to do. Corcoran listened in silence then turned to Kate.

"You've rented the cottage next door?" he asked, skepticism in his voice.

Next to her Trepalli bristled, but really, Kate couldn't blame Corcoran. How likely was it that she would just happen to rent the cottage next door to the home of a wanted fugitive?

"That's how I got involved in all this," she said. "My niece and I rented the cottage for the week but came home early. We've met Mrs. Olafson and she mentioned her son." She continued on to explain about the arson in Mendenhall and what Lucas Tormegev had revealed.

Corcoran's green eyes narrowed as he listened. Finally Kate fell silent and he spoke. "Nobody's said anything about a sister."

Kate nodded. "I know. Bergstrom and his sister ran away in 1985. A couple of years later, he was sentenced for aggravated sexual assault. No one's seen her since then and there's no record of her anywhere that I've been able to find, but Bergstrom told Tormegev that he was going home to find his mother *and* his sister."

She and Corcoran stared at each other for a moment after she finished talking. A shiver ran through her and she thought again about the crying she and Amanda had heard every night they stayed at the cottage. Could that have been Sarah Bergstrom? Was she a recluse in her own home? Was that the reason Sula Olafson never left the house?

That might also explain the light Kate had seen. If the upstairs of the Olafson house wasn't closed off, as Sula claimed, then the light could easily have been Sarah holding a candle at the window.

But that doesn't explain how the light traveled up the side of the house without a staircase...

Corcoran was a tall man, taller than Trepalli, and there was a sternness to him that spoke of experience rather than years. There was no gray in his sandy hair, though it was cut so short it was hard to tell.

"Has anyone spoken to Mrs. Olafson?" asked Trepalli, reminding everyone of his presence. "Have we checked her phone records? Maybe Bergstrom's been in touch with her."

Corcoran nodded. "We've checked her records. It was easy. She's made exactly one phone call in the last month, and received thirty, one for every day of the month, all from the same source."

Kate smiled. "Let me guess. The Pettersons."

A small smile tugged at the corner of Corcoran's mouth. "They look after her. They go see her at least once a week and check up by phone daily."

Kate nodded. "I've met them," she said. "Good people." She glanced at Bert. "Now, if you have no objection, we'd like to set ourselves up in the rental cottage."

Corcoran thought for a moment, then nodded slowly. "You should wait until full dark," he advised, looking at Bert. "You don't want him to see a uniform."

"Good point," said Bert.

"Chief," said Trepalli, "I should be there, too."

Kate looked at him. "Did you bring a sidearm?"

He opened his mouth to speak, then shook it. "Ma'am, did you?"

Kate smiled. "Yes, I did," she said. She had tucked it under her jacket in the Explorer. She didn't plan to confront a dangerous offender without protection.

Frustration wrote itself plain on Trepalli's features and before it could turn into stubbornness, Kate shook her head.

"I'm serious, Marco," she said. "We still don't know where Amanda is. I know her car isn't parked at the cottage, but it may be in Gimli. These folks," she swept her chin in an arc encompassing Corcoran and the other constables in the room, "are working to apprehend Bergstrom. We can't divert their efforts to finding Amanda when we don't even know if anything's wrong."

It killed her to say it. It was the rational way to proceed, no matter if all her instincts told her that Amanda was involved in the whole situation. She just couldn't figure out how, or why, and until she did, she refused to ask Corcoran to expend precious resources on what might be a wild goose chase.

Trepalli took a deep breath and nodded sharply. He was a smart boy. She was sure his instincts were screaming at him, too, but he saw the logic in her reasoning.

"Who is this Amanda?" asked Corcoran.

"My niece," said Kate before Trepalli could speak. "We can't find her in Mendenhall, and we're worried she may have returned to Gimli. To see Mrs. Olafson."

Corcoran nodded, though he clearly didn't understand the connection, and he didn't want to take the time to listen to a long explanation.

"I have one officer on patrol," he said. "Give me the model and make and the color, and I'll ask him to keep an eye out."

Kate hesitated but Bert stepped up. "That would be a great help," he said. "And with Trepalli also looking, we'll know soon enough if she's here. Her name is Amanda Coburn. She's 23 and drives a green Toyota Tercel. I don't have the plate number."

"I do," said Trepalli, fishing through his jeans pocket. He pulled out a slip of paper and rattled off the license plate number.

Kate looked down at the industrial gray linoleum on the floor. She didn't want to know how it was that Trepalli walked around with Amanda's license plate number in his pocket.

They exchanged cell phone numbers with Corcoran and obtained the numbers of his constables on stake-out. Even if they had access to radios, which they didn't, it wouldn't be wise to operate with radios on a stake-out. At least with cell phones they could text each other.

Kate and Bert left Marco behind in Kate's Explorer and drove to the cottage in the Honda. It was full dark and the moon was out. Was it only a few days ago that she had made this trip for the first time? It felt like months ago now. Kate rolled down the passenger window and took a deep breath of the night air. Roses. Mulch. Freshly cut grass.

They saw no sign of the Gimli officers on stakeout—which was as it should be. After a few minutes on Fireweed Road, she directed Bert to the right driveway.

They got out of the Honda and stood for a moment looking up at the night sky filled with stars and an almost-full moon.

Then Kate remembered Bert's uniform.

"Let's get inside," she said, and led the way to the front door. For the first time, she was grateful that there was no motion sensor on the lights, much as she had resented it when she first arrived.

The cottage was exactly as she and Amanda had left it. Kate went from room to room drawing the curtains before turning on lights, then she and Bert sat in the kitchen. He had found some generic coffee in the cupboard and now water dripped through the coffee maker.

If Amanda were here, she would be aghast that Bert could so blithely drink coffee that lived in a can in a cupboard, and Kate had to admit that compared to Bert, she was definitely a coffee snob.

Still, they would need the caffeine to get them through the night. So it didn't matter if the coffee came from a grocery store or a specialty store.

Sure. Keep telling yourself that.

"What's so funny?" asked Bert, catching sight of her smile.

She shook her head. "Nothing." She sat down at the table next to him and took his hand. "Thanks for coming with me."

He squeezed her hand and pulled her to him in a one-armed hug. She was engulfed in warm man scent and shivered as his body heat made her realize that she was chilled. She rested her forehead in the crook of his neck, content for the moment to just be.

"Wouldn't you rather be with Trepalli, searching for her?" he murmured against her hair.

Kate shook her head. She couldn't tell him how she knew, but she was convinced that Amanda was headed here to Sula Olafson's house. If she wasn't there already. But there was no car in Sula's driveway, and really, nowhere to hide a car on the point. Not easily, anyway.

It occurred to her that Amanda might have been in an accident and be lying in a ditch somewhere. But she and Trepalli would have seen the accident on their way in if it had happened on the Trans-Canada, or on the side highway to Gimli. She controlled an impulse to call in and find out from McKell if someone had reported an accident. He would call.

"Hey," said Bert softly, disengaging and pulling away from her. "Relax. We'll find her. She may have gone for a drive to clear her head. For all you know, she may be back home, wondering where the heck you are."

Kate smiled and to her horror, tears pricked her eyes. Dear lord, what was the matter with her? Imagining the worst and *crying* over it?

She stood up. "You're right. But since we're here, we may as well be of assistance." She described the back yard to him and warned him about the drop-off to the beach. "The staircase is to the far right."

Bert nodded and stood up, too. "It's dark, but with that moon, we won't have any cover on the beach. We'd better stay in the shadows in the yard and keep watch from there."

He was right. The clouds had moved on, leaving a mostly clear sky. The moon would be shining on the small strip of beach and any movement would be immediately visible. Her phone rang suddenly and she lunged for her coat hanging off the back of one of the kitchen chairs. Bert stepped back quickly to avoid being run over and she smiled apologetically as she fished the phone out.

"Williams," she said after pressing the on button.

"This is Staff Corcoran. Are you in place?"

"Just about," said Kate, trying to get her heartbeat under control. "We're going to set up in the back yard in case he tries a beach approach."

"Roger," said Corcoran. "Turn you phone to silent mode and I'll text you anything new." He paused for a moment. "Ma'am?"

"Yes, Staff Corcoran?"

"I'd appreciate it if you didn't have to fire your weapon in our jurisdiction."

"Understood, Staff Corcoran."

"And ma'am?"

"Yes, Staff Corcoran?"

"I'd appreciate it even more if you and DC Langdon didn't get hurt."

Kate smiled grimly. "So would we, Staff."

CHAPTER 16

S HE COULD feel the cold ground through her running shoes, and the dew had soaked the hem of her jeans. Despite having zipped up her jacket and stuck her hands in her pockets, humidity penetrated through the layers to lay clammy fingers on her flesh. She had tucked the nine mm into the back of her waistband and the handgun felt cold and uncomfortable.

She and Bert had staked out each end of the back yard. Kate sat in a wooden Adirondack chair in the moon shadow of the pine trees separating the cottage from the Olafson house, and Bert had settled in a plastic lawn chair by the stairs leading to the beach. She could barely make him out and she knew where to look. From the beach, they would be invisible.

From her vantage point, she couldn't actually *see* the beach, only the bushes that hid the edge of the drop-off, and beyond those, the surging and receding waters of Lake Winnipeg. From his angle, Bert had a clear view of the beach up to the Olafson property. Neither one of them had a good view of the beach in front of the Olafson house.

Moonlight struck the tops of the waves like metal striking flint. She could hear every wavelet as it hit the beach and the slide of wet sand as the wave receded. She would hear anyone walking down there long before she saw them.

One of Corcoran's men was set up on the point itself, in the little grove of trees she had discovered on her first day at the cottage. From there, he'd be able to watch the cottages across the tiny bay and the beach until it curved, hiding the Olafson house.

She shivered and wished she could get up and walk around. She had lost track of the time and didn't want to pull her cell phone out unnecessarily to look. The screen was way too bright, even inside her jacket. Corcoran checked in by text every hour, and there had been three checks so far. That made it past midnight. Or was it past one?

Where was Bergstrom? She knew in her gut he was heading for home, but what was taking him so long? They hadn't missed him, had they? Had he slipped in before they got their watchers on the ground? It could be. But how? She had seen recent pictures of him. He had prison tats crawling up his neck. There was no way anyone would pick him up hitchhiking. But there had been no vehicles reported stolen, and all the bus drivers had been canvassed and shown the pictures.

And what the hell was taking Trepalli so long? Gimli wasn't a big place. She could have walked the length and breadth of the town in the time it was taking him to find one green Tercel.

Her heart squeezed and she closed her eyes momentarily against the fear. Amanda. Where was the girl? Kate had called her at home and on the cell before she and Bert set up their stakeout, but she hadn't answered.

Mendenhall was on the lookout for her, and so was Gimli. If she was in either place, they would find her.

What would Rose say if she knew? That she should never have trusted Kate to look after her daughter?

Something had happened to Amanda. There was no way she would stay away this long without getting in touch. No matter how mad or upset she got, the girl wouldn't want Kate to worry. Not after last winter.

She almost groaned at the memory of Amanda lying so still in the snow, her blood running black in the moonlit night. It had only been a shoulder wound, but it could have been so much worse. Rose had forgiven Kate for that, but Kate knew the shooting had shaken Rose's confidence in her.

And now she had lost Rose's baby.

Her head snapped left before she knew she had heard something. She held her breath, trying to hear over the sudden pounding of her heart. Her hands tightened around the arms of the lawn chair and a sliver dug into her right hand as she prepared to launch herself out of the chair.

She waited, but the sound didn't repeat and she couldn't identify what had made it. There was no movement at the far end of the yard, where Bert was sitting. Had she imagined it?

Her cell phone rumbled against her chest and she jumped, and almost swore, biting down on her tongue just in time. She unzipped her jacket and pulled the phone out, keeping it well within the shelter of the jacket.

It was a text message from Trepalli: "Found car at rest stop on hwy. Flat tire. No sign of her. Be there soon."

What? Be *where* soon? He would blow their cover if he came to the cottage. Besides, where on the highway did he find Amanda's car? Were there any signs that someone else had been there? Signs of a struggle?

She was about to reply when the noise came again and she pressed the phone against her chest to hide its light.

She had definitely heard something. Something sliding on the sand.

A shiver shot up her scalp as she thought of snakes slithering on the beach. A movement caught her eye. Bert had stood up.

Slipping the phone back in her inside jacket pocket, Kate stood up, too, and edged closer to the bushes at the top of the little drop-off. Was someone out there?

She caught a movement down on the dark beach by the Olafson house, more a suggestion than an actual movement, and

THE WEEPING WOMAN   149

her eyes strained to see past the shivering bushes to the dark shadows beyond. After a moment she finally made out shapes.

Someone was on the beach, pulling a heavy rowboat toward the water. She caught her breath and ran as silently as she could toward Bert and the stairs leading down to the beach. He was waiting for her and caught her with an arm around her waist, preventing her from taking the stairs at a run.

"Wait," he whispered. "I texted the others."

But Kate couldn't wait. Whoever was out there was pulling the boat toward the water. They had to stop him before he disappeared into the night.

"He's getting away," she whispered back fiercely, and disentangled herself from his arm to fly down the stairs. She hit the sand at the bottom with a thump and immediately took off running toward the Olafson beach, a hundred feet away.

The dark figure was shaped weirdly, as if one shoulder was much bigger than the other. It lurched toward the water, pulling the rowboat behind.

Eighty feet.

It took Kate a couple of seconds to realize he was carrying someone over his shoulder, and although she couldn't see, she could make an educated guess about who it was.

Seventy feet.

Bert pounded along behind her and she turned her head toward him, "He's got Mrs. Olafson!" Then she turned back to the dark figure and, using all the authority she could muster while she was out of breath, yelled, "Bergstrom! Stop!"

He ignored her completely.

Sixty feet.

He was already at the water's edge and with one powerful surge, he shoved the rowboat into the water.

Fifty feet.

He pulled Mrs. Olafson off his shoulder and deposited her gently onto the bottom of the boat.

Forty feet.

But as he did, the hood slipped away from Mrs. Olafson's head to reveal not white hair in a bun, but gleaming blonde hair in a ponytail.

"Amanda!" screamed Kate.

Thirty feet.

Her heart slammed against her rib cage, as much from the knowledge that she wasn't going to make it as from exertion. Then Bert pulled ahead of her, his arms pumping, his feet landing like pile drivers. She got a glimpse of his face as he passed her. His lips were parted in a snarl and his teeth were clenched.

"Bergstrom!" she shouted and the figure at the rowboat finally paused. Then, as if realizing how little time he had, he gave the boat another mighty shove and followed it into the water.

She pushed herself to run faster. That son of a bitch was taking Amanda! She wanted to scream and yell at him, but her breath was coming in great rasps and she couldn't spare the energy.

The rowboat was now floating free of the beach and Bergstrom swung a leg over the side and prepared to haul himself in. They were going to lose him.

And then Bert launched himself off the beach, his powerful leg muscles propelling him over the intervening water.

"Bert, no!" Kate shouted. What did he think he was doing? He couldn't swim worth a damn!

He almost made it. His fingers actually caught the prow of the rowboat, but then Bergstrom scrambled into the boat, making it rock, and Bert lost his grip. He surged out of the water to try again, but by then the water was almost over his head and he had nothing against which to brace himself.

Kate struggled out of her jacket as she ran, dropping it onto the beach. She pulled the nine mm out of her waistband and tossed it onto the sand.

Bergstrom had managed to gain his seat and was now moving away from the beach. Just before she plunged into the cold water of Lake Winnipeg, Kate had time to wonder at the eerie silence that had descended on the scene. She could see the oars dipping powerfully into the water and should have heard the creaking of the oarlocks, the water dripping off the oars. She could see Bert frantically trying to catch the rowboat and should have heard him yelling. But all she could hear was her labored breathing.

Then she dove into the water and all thinking stopped. She pushed against the waves with her powerful crawl, mindful of the need to keep her breathing under control. Every time she turned her head, she saw the rowboat pulling farther away with its precious cargo.

She had to catch up, had to keep him from throwing Amanda overboard.

For she had caught a glimpse of Daniel Bergstrom's face as he pulled against the oars, and it was a face filled with madness.

She wanted to scream for help, for another boat, but she couldn't spare the breath. She prayed that Bert had managed to get out but she didn't dare turn to check. She had to keep the boat in sight. Bergstrom was taking Amanda farther and farther away, gradually fading away into the night-shrouded lake.

Faster!

She redoubled her efforts, focusing on keeping the rowboat in sight and trying to catch up to it. She caught a mouthful of water and almost choked, coughing and struggling to keep afloat. By the time she had caught her breath, she could no longer see the rowboat.

And then, finally, she heard a sound that she hadn't produced. The sound of a woman crying.

A massive shiver shook her. Her running shoes were heavy but they provided some measure of protection from the cold. Her jeans, however, constricted her movements. She had to keep moving or she would go hypothermic. But in which direction? She strained to hear the sound of the rowboat, but the only sound that reached her was that unearthly weeping. She glanced over her shoulder and saw the Olafson house with lights ablaze like a beacon and to her immense relief, she saw figures running on the beach, and—oh, blessed relief!—moonlight on a wet paddle as a canoe came surging through the water toward her.

Re-oriented, she turned her back on the beach and struck out at a ninety degree angle. Bergstrom had been heading straight out and hadn't deviated in the time she had followed him. She would just keep going until she heard him or saw him.

Please God, don't let me be too late.

And then, as if in answer, she saw him. Or rather she saw a paler shade against the inky darkness. And then she heard water lapping against wood. She was getting closer. He must have stopped. She had to be silent but she was shaking in the water, her energy all but sapped.

She forced herself to swim closer. She was only ten feet away now. She became aware that Bergstrom was standing up in the rowboat, his face turned toward shore.

Kate could still hear the crying. A trick of acoustics made it sound like it was right next to her, and if she hadn't been so thoroughly chilled already, she would have gotten goose bumps. *Swim,* she told herself. *Swim while you still can.*

Just then a light appeared to her right. It swept past her and found the rowboat. It took her a second to realize that it was a powerful flashlight.

"Daniel Bergstrom!"

Relief surged through her. That was Bert's voice. She glanced over her shoulder and saw the canoe less than thirty feet away. Still too far.

"Stay where you are," ordered Bert.

Kate wished he was talking to her, but she was pretty sure he hadn't seen her. She turned back to the rowboat and to her horror, she saw that Bergstrom had draped Amanda's still form over the side of the craft.

"No!" she screamed, but it was too late. Amanda slid soundlessly into the dark waters of the lake.

With a last burst of energy, she dove after her niece, holding her hands out in front of her and kicking with all her might. She should be able to catch Amanda before she sank too deep. But the water was so dark, so disorienting...

Kate swept her arms out, hoping against hope to catch Amanda's ponytail, or snag her hoodie, but all she felt was water and more water. She swam deeper, struggling against the desperate need to breathe, aware that she was almost at the end of her strength. But she couldn't give up, couldn't leave Amanda to drown.

She swept the water with her hands, gritting her teeth against her body's raging need to breathe, and then she saw a pale oval and *reached* even as she recognized that it was a face, and then her hand felt wet, heavy fabric and she closed her fingers around it and hauled.

She kicked upward, or what she hoped was upward, only one thought in mind, to reach the surface and *breathe!* She glanced down to make sure she wouldn't lose her grip and saw a stranger looking straight at her.

Startled, Kate let go, then panicked. Was that Amanda she had let go? It hadn't looked like her, but Bergstrom hadn't gone in, so it *had* to be her! She flailed around, trying desperately to find the girl again, then a cold hand clamped around her wrist and Kate got a good look at the face swimming up to her.

It was Sarah Bergstrom.

Kate opened her mouth to scream, only to swallow water. She struggled upward, trying to free herself of the vise-like grip, kicking harder, a mindless animal concerned only with survival.

And then there was a glimmering light and she shot past the killing barrier of water and into air.

A hand found her free arm and she would have screamed except that she was too busy coughing and trying to breathe.

"I've got you," said Bert roughly, grabbing her under the armpits. "Hang on, Katie. We've got you."

CHAPTER 17

THE TEA was much too sweet, and it was too hot, but Kate cradled the mug and sipped cautiously. It was hard to keep from spilling the liquid when she was still shivering so much.

Reaction, Bert had said. Hypothermia, she thought.

She glanced across the table at Amanda. Even huddled under two blankets and with her hair pulled into a rat's tail rather than a ponytail, the girl was a wonderful sight. Until you looked into her eyes.

Trepalli hovered over her even worse than Bert had hovered over Kate. She had finally given him the "look," the one that said, "You're making me look bad in front of the others" and he had backed off, but not far. He was helping Mrs. Olafson with making sandwiches and more tea for the searchers, but every few seconds he glanced back to make sure she was still there.

Above the old-fashioned enamel farm sink, the frilly yellow curtains had been pulled open and now revealed Mrs. Olafson's shabby back yard lit with powerful portable lights. Beyond the beach—invisible from their point of view—there was a hub of activity, with officers and powerful speed boats slowly criss-crossing the lake in front of the house.

They still hadn't found Bergstrom, although Trepalli and Bert both assured her that he had drowned. They had brought the row-boat back in when the RCMP cruiser arrived, but it revealed nothing. Mrs. Olafson had confirmed that her son must have pulled it from the side of the house, where it had been for over twenty years. Bert had said it was a miracle the thing hadn't sunk while Bergstrom was rowing it out.

Kate glanced at Mrs. Olafson's back. The woman worked steadily, methodically, making food with the little bit she had on hand. It occurred to Kate that she should call the Pettersons and ask them to come by. Mrs. Olafson should not be alone.

No one had questioned the woman yet. Or Amanda, for that matter.

Kate hadn't realized until later, but Trepalli had been in the canoe with Bert. The boy had been in the water, hauling Amanda up while Bert was busy hauling Kate in. And then Trepalli had performed mouth-to-mouth on Amanda while Bert frantically paddled to shore. The waiting constables had hauled the canoe onto shore and pulled Amanda out to lay her on the sand.

There followed the longest few minutes of Kate's life, as Trepalli continued mouth-to-mouth resuscitation until Amanda finally coughed and threw up lake water. Then the emergency medical services crew arrived and hauled them into Mrs. Olafson's house to get checked out.

Kate closed her eyes against sudden tears. She had almost lost Amanda.

A warm hand landed on her shoulder and squeezed. "You heard the EMS guys," said Bert softly. "Drink. It'll warm you up." He placed a plate with a cheese and tomato sandwich in front of her. "And while you're at it, eat."

He looked down at her, his copper-penny eyes warm with concern and love. She tried to smile at him but her gaze returned of its own volition to Amanda.

The girl had spoken barely a dozen words since she'd been pulled out of the water, and those were mostly in answer to the

EMS guy's questions.

Mrs. Olafson had found them both dry clothes. Kate was pretty sure her clothes—a pair of trousers that were a little tight on the waist and so long they had to be rolled up and a turtleneck and heavy sweater—belonged to Mrs. Olafson herself, but she brought Amanda a pair of acid-washed, artfully ripped jeans and an oversized flannel shirt that she wore over a plain white tee-shirt.

Sarah's clothes.

It was hard to think of Sarah Bergstrom as anything but the young woman she had been when she disappeared. In reality, if she had lived, Sarah would have been Kate's contemporary.

A shudder shook Kate and she closed her eyes only to open them again when Sarah's face floated up out of the darkness behind her eyelids. She had imagined it. It was Amanda she had grabbed, not Sarah.

She swallowed more tea and pulled the blanket closer around her shoulders. It was time for some answers.

At that moment, a door opened somewhere in the bowels of the house and they all turned toward the hallway in surprise. The distant door closed and footsteps made their way from the dark hallway toward the kitchen.

Suddenly, Bert and Trepalli were standing side by side, blocking the access to the kitchen. And just as suddenly, they parted to allow Alice and Jakob Petterson to enter.

Kate stared at Bert. What the hell was that about? And then she knew. They'd lied to her and Amanda. They didn't know where Bergstrom was, and they were worried that he had swum to shore and would come back to finish what he had started.

Which was what, exactly?

Mrs. Petterson's hair flowed down her back in a thick, dishevelled braid. She wore a pair of green pants and a heavy corduroy shirt in a shade of gray that did not go well with her pants.

"Sula!" Alice Petterson went straight to her friend and wrapped her arms around her. As if she had been waiting for just that, Mrs.

Olafson lay her head on Alice's shoulder and began to weep.

Jakob Petterson watched the two women gravely for a moment, his bald head gleaming in the overhead light. He wore jeans and a white cable knit sweater, but when she glanced down at his feet, she saw that he wore slippers. Not as calm and collected as he looked.

The old man turned to look around the room, his gaze taking in Kate and lingering for a long moment on Amanda before landing on Trepalli, then Bert. He nodded to Bert, then glanced out the kitchen window.

"So," he said heavily. "The prodigal son returned." His expression was stern and there were deep grooves on either side of his mouth.

"What's your name, sir?" asked Bert in his cop's voice.

Mr. Petterson looked down at Bert, frowning. Kate stood up.

"Bert, this is Jakob Petterson and his wife, Alice. They are friends of Mrs. Olafson's." She turned to Mr. Petterson. "How did you know?"

Sadness swept over the old man, bowing his shoulders and making his mouth droop.

"Officer Corcoran called us," he said.

Kate nodded. "I'm glad you're here," she said gently.

At last Bert stepped aside and let the old man go to his wife and their friend.

Kate went over to Amanda and tilted her chin up. To her surprise, Amanda met her gaze with a smile.

"I'm fine, Aunt Kate," she said softly.

"Well, I'm not," said Kate caustically. She turned to survey the room. "In fact, I think it's time someone told me what happened here tonight. Starting with what the hell *you* were doing here." She looked pointedly at Amanda, who ducked her head. Trepalli immediately went to stand behind her and put his hands on her shoulders, frowning over Amanda's head at Kate.

"Oh, don't even," she warned him. "You were worried sick,

too." She looked down at her niece. "What happened to your car? How did you get from the highway to here?"

Amanda sighed. "I got a flat tire, and my spare was flat, too," she said. "I was only a mile or so from Sula's so I decided to walk. Daniel saw me walking on the side of the road and stopped." She looked down at her lap. "He forced me into his car. He tied me up and broke into an empty cottage. Then he waited until it was dark."

A silence descended on the group as they considered what could have happened. They already knew that besides trying to drown her, Daniel Bergstrom hadn't harmed Amanda, but Kate would never know why not. Was it because she reminded him too much of his sister?

"Why didn't you call for help?" asked Bert.

"Because I'd left my cell phone at home," Amanda told him sheepishly. "I knew Aunt Kate would try to stop me if I told her I was coming here."

"Why come here in the first place?" demanded Kate.

Amanda looked around and her gaze found Mrs. Olafson's. The old woman disentangled herself from her friend's arms and wiped her face. Her white hair was still in a bun, but the bun was askew, and tendrils had escaped and now floated around her face. She wore black trousers that had been in style forty years ago, and a man's white shirt open to reveal a gray turtleneck. The resemblance to Katherine Hepburn was uncanny.

"She came because Sarah wanted her to come," she said.

There was a long silence in the kitchen while everyone looked at the old woman.

It was Trepalli who finally broke it.

"Sarah, your daughter?" he said.

Mrs. Olafson nodded.

"Is she here?" he asked uncertainly. He glanced at the ceiling and despite herself, Kate glanced up, too. Had Sarah Bergstrom been here all these years?

"Not anymore," said Amanda, startling Kate.

What was that supposed to mean?

"What do you mean?" asked Trepalli. He moved away from Amanda so that he could look at her. "She *was* here?"

Amanda turned to Mrs. Olafson. Before either one could respond, Mrs. Petterson spoke up.

"No," she said firmly, wrapping an arm around Sula's back. "Sarah ran away with Daniel in '85."

Sula's chin lifted but she didn't say anything. Her eyes filled with tears again.

Bert sighed. "All right. It's late and we're all exhausted. Corcoran and I have assigned a few men to watch this house and the cottage next door. Tomorrow we'll sort this all out and make statements."

Kate wanted to argue that she still had many questions, but as if his words had triggered it, a wave of exhaustion swept over her, draining her of strength and willpower.

Tomorrow, then.

CHAPTER 18

IT WAS six o'clock before Kate stumbled out of bed, and then only because she heard voices. A glance out the window told her that morning was well under way and she should be, too. Her clothes were folded on the chair by the door, though she couldn't remember putting them in the dryer. Mrs. Olafson's clothes were nowhere to be seen. She dressed quickly and padded bare-footed into the kitchen, which was empty.

The wonderful aroma of fresh coffee enticed, but she ignored it in favor of going to the sun porch door.

Bert looked up as she walked in and Trepalli paused, his hand on the door knob, as if he had been about to go out. Bert smiled and opened his mouth to say something when his gaze caught in her hair. He paused for a split second and Kate's hands went up to her hair. She combed through it self-consciously, aware that Trepalli was still staring.

In spite of everything she had slept well enough, but thoughts of Bergstrom had floated through her dreams all night. She studied Bert's face for a moment, then turned to look at Trepalli, who was standing by the door that led to the back yard.

"How did Bergstrom get to the beach?" she asked. "We had men watching. How did he get to the house without being seen?"

"And a good morning to you, too," said Bert with a smile. He gave her hair another quick look and then looked away. Good grief. Trepalli's reaction she could understand, but Bert had seen her many times in the morning.

"Mr. Petterson told me last night that the only watcher Bergstrom would've had to watch out for was the one on the point. Once he got down to the beach level, all he had to do was stay close to the cliff and no one would see him."

"But he was carrying Amanda!"

Trepalli's mouth tightened. He nodded. "Ma'am, he grew up here. He would have known how to stay out of sight."

Kate glanced at Bert and caught him in a yawn. She took in the bags under his eyes.

"You didn't sleep at all, did you?" she asked accusingly.

Bert shrugged and Trepalli just grinned.

"What happened to the unis stationed outside?" she asked. Bert had told her there'd be one uniformed officer out front and one out back.

"They were there," Trepalli assured her.

Kate glanced from one smug face to the other and almost shook her head. They didn't trust anyone else to look out for their girl-friends. A small part of her felt manipulated but she had trouble keeping the smile off her face.

Honestly.

There were two full cups of coffee on the table in front of the couch. Kate looked up at Trepalli. "Where were you going?"

"They think they've found him," said Bert. "Marco was going next door to help."

The sudden relief was so great that Kate leaned against the door jamb for support. "I'm going, too," she said grimly.

"Me, too," said Amanda. Kate turned to see her niece standing behind her, wearing her red hoodie and a pair of jeans. Like Kate, the girl was bare-footed. Her hair was down around her shoul-ders and dishevelled, but unlike Kate, it looked fetching. Without a word, Kate gave Amanda a fierce hug then let her go. She turned to the two men.

"Let's go."

Trepalli glanced at Bert, who got up stiffly from the couch.

"Let Marco go ahead," he suggested. "You two put something on your feet." He gave Kate a sly glance. "And comb your hair."

* * *

The body was laid out on the beach in front of Mrs. Olafson's house, covered by a bright blue plastic tarp. Mr. and Mrs. Petterson stood with Sula Olafson in front of the body, shoulders touching. Mrs. Olafson looked as if she hadn't slept in days, but her hair was neat and her clothes fresh. Staff Corcoran stood a little ways from the group, watching them. A young RCMP constable unknown to Kate knelt at the head of the body, watching Corcoran.

To Kate's surprise, the RCMP boat was still anchored off the shore, maybe a hundred feet out. There was a constable in it, wearing a bright orange flotation vest.

"Are you ready?" asked Corcoran softly.

Kate, Bert, Trepalli, and Amanda turned as one to look at Mrs. Olafson, who nodded once. Her eyes, though bloodshot, were dry.

Corcoran nodded to the constable and the young man pulled the tarp away from the body.

According to his file, Daniel Bergstrom was fifty-three, but in death he looked younger. The water had plumped up the deep grooves in his forehead and cheeks. He had high cheekbones and a good mouth marred by a fresh, three-inch scar that pulled his upper lip into a perpetual sneer. The scar hadn't been noted in the file.

His hair was still blonde, with a lot of gray, and it was in a brush cut. He wore a navy sweatshirt with Adidas embroidered over the breast. Tattoos crawled out of his sweatshirt and up his neck, stopping shy of the jawline.

They were probably prison tats, but she didn't feel like examining them too closely. It looked like Daniel Bergstrom had embraced prison life fully.

"Yes, that's my son," said Sula Olafson clearly. She stood straight and there was something firm and unyielding about her. Kate couldn't interpret the expression on her face. She glanced at Amanda but her niece was looking at the RCMP boat, her mouth tight.

"Thank you," said Corcoran, and with a nod to the constable, ordered him to pull the tarp up.

"What's going to happen to the body?" asked Mrs. Olafson.

Kate glanced at Bert, who blinked in surprise. The question seemed devoid of emotion, as if she were talking about a side of beef.

Corcoran seemed nonplussed, too. "Ah... Well, it will be sent to Winnipeg for an autopsy, ma'am. Afterward, we can send it wherever you like for disposal."

"I don't want him back," said Sula Olafson clearly. "Dispose of him as you will."

Alice and Jakob Petterson glanced at each other but said nothing. Corcoran cleared his throat and nodded. "As you wish. I'll make sure you get the appropriate paperwork."

"What are they looking for?" asked Trepalli. He was looking at the RCMP boat. Kate followed his gaze and studied the boat, too. For the first time, she realized that there were still divers in the water. She turned to Corcoran who glanced uncertainly at Mrs. Olafson.

"One of the divers thought he saw something down there," he said.

Well, that was evasive.

Kate glanced around the tableau. Everyone had puzzled expressions, save for Mrs. Olafson and Amanda, who were staring at each other.

"What is it?" asked Kate, reaching for Amanda's hand. "What's the matter?"

Amanda turned to look at her but before she could say anything, a whistle sounded from the boat and they all turned to see the constable in the boat holding his arm up high and looking at them.

"They've found her," whispered Amanda, and a shiver ran up Kate's scalp.

CHAPTER 19

OVER TWENTY-FIVE years in the water." Bert shook his head. "There's not much left to identify her."

Kate nodded. They had sent Trepalli and Amanda inside with the Pettersons and Mrs. Olafson. There was no need for any of them to see this. What remained of the body had been placed in a body-shaped cage; the diver had then swum to shore, dragging it behind him. When they finally hauled the cage up onto another tarp, it became clear why the body had never surfaced. Three old-fashioned cement blocks—the kind used in retaining walls and basement walls when Kate was growing up—were tied with chains around the corpse's neck, waist, and feet.

There was no flesh left. One skeletal hand was gone, detached by the action of the water or scavengers. The tattered remains of a dress still covered the skeleton but it was hard to tell what colour it had been. Blue, maybe? With flowers? If there had been shoes, they were long gone, but a black plastic belt hung to the skeleton's hips, held in place by fabric loops in the waistband.

Corcoran finished taking pictures and straightened up with a sigh.

"Whoever she is," he said, "somebody didn't want her coming back up." He nodded to the cement blocks.

"Do you think it's Sarah Bergstrom?" asked Bert, but he was

looking at Kate.

The sun was beginning to make itself felt but she didn't remove her jacket. There was no doubt in her mind that this was Sarah Bergstrom, and that her brother Daniel had dumped her body into the lake all those years ago, just as he had dumped Amanda into the lake last night.

Kate's breath quickened as the memory of Sarah Bergstrom's face swimming up out of the dark depths flashed through her mind.

Oxygen deprivation had confused her so that she transposed the image of the young woman she had seen in the newspaper photo with Amanda's face. And the crying?

And the light...?

Kate shivered and Bert looked at her in surprise.

"We may never know for sure," she said. "But it would explain why she never got in touch with her mother."

Corcoran nodded. "I think it's time we asked some questions," he said. He glanced around the beach and called one of his constables, who came over at a run.

"Jason, stand watch until the coroner's crew gets here. Don't forget to obtain a custody report."

The constable nodded and Corcoran, Kate, and Bert trudged up the beach to the narrow, steep path that led up to Sula Olafson's back yard. They wound their way through overgrown grass and past ancient garden beds and climbed the back stairs to the porch. Trepalli opened the door for them and they trooped into the kitchen.

Alice and Jakob Petterson stood side by side in the kitchen, arms crossed and staring at the floor. Mrs. Petterson looked up when they entered, a question in her eyes.

"Who is it?" asked Trepalli.

Bert sighed. He glanced at the older couple and clearly revised what he had been about to say. "Unknown for now," he said.

Trepalli nodded to show he understood.

"Where's Amanda?" asked Kate, looking around.

"In the parlor with Sula," said Jakob Petterson.

Kate was already walking down the hallway toward the parlor but when she arrived at the doorway, she stopped. Amanda and Sula Olafson were holding each other tightly and weeping.

Without a word, she crept back the way she had come and left them alone.

* * *

"The moment he found out she was adopted, he changed."

They had all crowded into the parlor: Kate, Amanda, Trepalli, Bert, Corcoran, the Pettersons, and Mrs. Olafson. A young constable stood in the corner, out of the way, and took notes.

"Who was adopted?" asked Bert. He had given Kate the needle-point covered armchair and now he perched on the arm, clearly trying not to put his entire weight on it. Kate didn't blame him. All the furniture in the room looked fragile, as if a puff of wind would blow it all to dust.

"Sarah," said Amanda. She sat on the settee, next to Mrs. Olafson, holding her hand. Trepalli hovered next to her, clearly unable to sit down. He might as well not have been there for all the attention Amanda gave him.

"He was fourteen when we told Sarah. She was fifteen and wanted to know why she didn't look like me or her father. Until then, Daniel had been... a handful, but she had kept him under control." Sula Olafson looked at the empty fireplace, not seeing it, her words taking her back to old memories.

"She was such a good child," she whispered.

"She was," agreed Alice Petterson, sitting on Sula's other side. She reached over and patted her friend's free hand. "Everybody loved her."

"Unlike Daniel," said Sula Olafson sadly. "He was constantly in trouble, but we thought it was just the normal troubles of a rambunctious child. And Sarah always kept an eye on him. We never worried. Not really."

She fell into a silence that seemed as if it would stretch on for days.

"What changed?" asked Kate finally. Inside her running shoes, her feet were getting cold. The runners hadn't dried properly from their soak in the lake the night before, and now the dampness was transferring through her socks and into her feet.

"He changed," said Sula. "He became more secretive. He would disappear for hours at a time and no one would know where he had gone. As he grew older, it became worse. At first he shunned Sarah, treating her as if she didn't exist. And then, that changed, too." Her voice trailed off and she looked down at her lap. Her hand tightened on Amanda's.

"He took an unnatural interest in his sister," said Jakob Petterson suddenly. He stood at the other end of the settee, a twin bookend to Trepalli. Unlike Trepalli, however, he stood very still, as if his feet were rooted to the oak floor. Alice looked up at her husband, her face sad.

Corcoran cleared his throat from his position in the other armchair. "Unnatural?" he asked softly.

Jakob nodded sharply. "Eventually, he began to spy on her. When she was bathing. Or sleeping. He followed her. We all noticed before Sarah did, and when Jonas asked her about it, she even defended her brother. Jonas spoke to the boy but by then he was eighteen and bigger than his father. There was nothing they could do short of kicking him out of the house, and they were not ready for that." He shook his head and looked at Amanda. "And then the incidents began in town."

"What incidents?" asked Trepalli.

Bert leaned over and whispered in Kate's ear. "Who's Jonas?"

Kate whispered back, "Daniel's father."

Jakob glanced at them but answered Trepalli. "Girls' underthings were stolen," he said grimly. "At first we all thought it was a prank by the town boys. But then the break-ins started and then, one night, a girl was raped in her bed, while her parents were at the neighbor's." He took a deep breath, as if the tale had exhausted him. Alice took his hand and squeezed. Then she turned to the group and resumed Jakob's tale.

"Nobody knew who was responsible." She glanced at Sula. "Then Sula found where he had hidden the underwear he had stolen. Jonas was away on one of his business trips, and Sarah was in town, and so Sula confronted him." She, too, fell silent, as if she couldn't bear to recount what came next.

One by one, even the constable in the corner, they all turned to look at Sula Olafson. Finally she raised her head and looked at Amanda.

"He struck me," she said softly. "I fell unconscious. It was hours before I woke up, and it was dark. By then, they were gone. There was a note on the kitchen table in his handwriting. He told me that they were leaving and not to look for them, that they never wanted to see us again." Her voice broke on the last word and she looked down at her lap and at Amanda's hand clutched in hers.

"Is that why you cry every night?" asked Kate suddenly. Everyone turned to look at her in surprise. "At one-fifteen?" She felt the heat rising in her cheeks. It really did sound ridiculous.

Sula Olafson just stared at Kate. "What do you mean?"

"I heard it, too," said Amanda, to Kate's intense relief. "From the first night we arrived."

Sula was shaking her head, clearly puzzled. "Last night was the first time I've cried in years."

Kate and Amanda glanced at each other, then away. They couldn't both be crazy.

"Go on..." pressed Kate, turning to look at the old woman.

Sula Olafson's breathing quickened. "It was late when I came to. None of their clothing was missing. If they had planned this, why hadn't they packed? I never saw my children again. Until today."

"The police searched," said Jakob, taking up the story. "But there was no sign of them until we learned, many years later, that Daniel was in prison for raping a girl. But of Sarah, there was no sign."

"Everybody said she was too ashamed to come home," said Alice, looking at her friend. "But you always knew, didn't you?"

Sula nodded and only now could Kate see the tears slowly coursing down her cheeks. "She would never have left me without a word, without trying to reach me. I knew that something had happened to her."

Kate swallowed a lump in her throat and glanced at Amanda. The girl was crying, too.

"That's why you never left, isn't it?" asked Amanda.

Sula sighed and nodded. She freed her hand and wiped her cheek. "I knew that one day he would come back. I knew he couldn't stay away from her forever." She looked at Amanda. "And then you came." She touched Amanda's cheek.

"The resemblance is uncanny," said Jakob. "Save that Sarah was dark and your Amanda is so fair."

"Yes," said Sula. She patted Amanda's cheek. "You look so much like her," she said with a watery smile. "You even have the same smile. It was almost as if she had returned to me."

Kate shifted uncomfortably in her chair. She didn't see it, this resemblance they were talking about. Not from the newspaper picture she had seen, anyway.

Something had changed between Sula Olafson and Amanda. Despite their obvious closeness, Kate no longer sensed the same link that had been present earlier. It was as if now that Sula knew where her daughter was, she could see that Amanda was a different person.

"Why kill her?" Kate asked finally.

There was a long silence while everyone waited for Sula to answer, but to Kate's surprise, it was Amanda who spoke.

"Because she wouldn't go with him," she said softly. "And he couldn't bear that."

CHAPTER 20

KATE STOOD in her darkened dining room, holding her wine glass in front of her, and stared out at the illuminated deck. Dan Boychuk wandered past the half-open French doors, batting away mosquitos and talking to Samantha Paterson's husband about Mendenhall United, the men's soccer team. Kate had last seen Paterson helping herself to a pastry filled with spinach and cream cheese that Amanda had concocted for the party.

The lights on the deck blinded her to the night sky, but it was another clear, cool night. It would be cooler still in Gimli.

She sighed softly. They had left Sula Olafson yesterday in the capable hands of the Pettersons. Kate suspected that the Olafson house would be sold now, or at least closed up, and that Sula would end up living with her friends.

Kate couldn't imagine Sula wanting to stay in the home that had witnessed her son murder her daughter, and over thirty years later, her son's attempted murder of Amanda.

No one seemed to know why Daniel Bergstrom had wanted to drown Amanda. There *was* no reason, except that Amanda reminded Sula Olafson of her daughter, Sarah. While Kate couldn't see the resemblance, everyone else seemed to think the resemblance was uncanny.

Maybe Daniel Bergstrom, already on the edge, had seen Amanda on the road and thought Sarah had come back. They would never know, would they?

Kate wished she could pinpoint exactly when Amanda had started acting strange on their little holiday. Was it before or after they learned about Sula and her sad story? Why had Amanda *identified* with the dead girl?

A burst of raucous laughter in the kitchen caused her to turn her head but she didn't leave her spot. She had decided to throw an impromptu birthday party for Amanda. She had wanted something fun, something *normal* to end this holiday from hell. Everyone from the station had shown up, except for Ben Friesen, who wasn't yet back from Japan. Even the officers on duty had spelled each other to come toast Amanda.

Most of the activity was in the living room and in the kitchen, and on the deck. Someone had changed the music to something with a hip hop beat but it was hard to hear over the ebb and flow of conversation.

She raised the wine glass to her lips and sipped. Amanda was out there in the dark, with Trepalli. Kate had seen them slip away fifteen minutes ago, heading for the back of the yard. If she strained, she could just make out two dark figures at the back of the yard, heads close together.

"Hey," said Bert, coming up behind her. "What are you doing here all alone?" He slipped his arms around her waist and pulled her to him. She rested her back against his solid chest and tried not to cry.

"I think she's leaving," she said softly.

Bert's breath ruffled her hair by her temple. Finally he pulled away and turned her to face him.

"Why do you say that?" he asked. "Did she say something?"

Kate shook her head and took another sip of the Chardonnay. "No, not yet. I suspect she's telling Trepalli right now, though."

No, Amanda hadn't said anything. She hadn't needed to.

The moment they'd arrived back home yesterday, a small part of Kate had known. Amanda had seemed... at peace. Yes, that was the word. As if she had made a decision.

"What do you suppose that crying was?" she asked suddenly.

In the light from the deck, Bert looked perplexed. "What crying?"

"That night." And every night she'd stayed at the cottage. "The night he tried to drown Amanda. When I was swimming out there—didn't you hear a woman crying?" The memory of that unearthly crying as she fought to reach Amanda would stay with her a long, long time.

Bert was shaking his head. "All I could hear was me shouting at Bergstrom to stop."

Frustration welled up in her. Nobody else had heard the crying, not Bert, not even Mrs. Olafson. Nobody but her and Amanda. And nobody else had seen that mysterious light climbing up the side of the Olafson house, either.

Let it go, she finally told herself. *Let it go before it drives you crazy.*

"Where's the birthday girl?" shouted McKell from the kitchen. "It's time for birthday cake!"

In the ensuing hubbub, Amanda returned to the house to cheers and teasing. McKell lit the candles and everyone crowded around and sang Happy Birthday while Amanda blew out the candles.

Kate cheered along with everyone when Amanda blew out all the candles but her gaze had swept the crowded kitchen and hadn't found Trepalli.

When the noise level died down enough for her to be heard, Amanda took a deep breath.

"Listen, everyone," she said. "I have something to say." She took a deep breath. "I've decided to go back to Montreal."

Kate's heart squeezed and she felt tears prick her eyes but she was ready when Amanda's gaze found hers. She read the apology in her niece's face and nodded her understanding. She knew this wasn't how Amanda would have chosen to tell her, but with all her friends from the station gathered in one spot, it was too good an opportunity to pass up.

The room erupted in questions and Kate felt McKell's gaze on her but she didn't take her attention away from Amanda. Next to her, Bert reached for her hand and squeezed it.

"You'll have to let her go," he said softly, not looking at her.

"I know," whispered Kate. "I know."

CHAPTER 21

O N MONDAY morning, Rose called her on the office land line.

"She's here," she said without a greeting.

Kate closed her eyes against the sudden tears. It seemed she teared up at nothing these days.

"She made good time," she said gruffly. "No problems?"

"No problems," said Rose. And then she remained silent.

Kate listened to her sister breathing at the other end of the line and considered all the things she had done wrong. It didn't matter that she'd had very little control over any of the events that had transpired over the past week. The only thing that mattered was that Amanda had almost died again.

Last February she had been shot by a madwoman, and now she had been attacked by a madman. Kate had been the one to place her niece in danger both times. And now Amanda had moved back to Montreal. It had taken surprisingly little time for her to pack up the little Tercel and leave.

Now there was an emptiness in Kate's home and a hole in her heart.

And her sister was furious with her.

"Oh God, Rose," she whispered. "I'm so sorry."

Rose remained silent for a moment longer, then blew out her

breath in a long, ragged sigh. "I know. And I know none of it is your fault," she added. "Amanda told me the whole story."

She fell silent again and Kate searched for words that would cross the void and reach her sister. Had she lost her sister as well as her niece?

"She was unhappy here these last few weeks," she admitted painfully. "Even before this whole... thing... happened. I think she realized she had made a mistake coming here."

To her surprise, Rose laughed. "Oh, no. It had nothing to do with that," she assured Kate. "I knew the minute I saw her. Some boy was making her unhappy."

Trepalli. Kate's hand tightened around the receiver and she turned to study the view outside her window, but it did nothing to calm her. Damn the boy!

"I'm sorry about all of it," she said inadequately. "I don't know how you do it, Rose. I guess it's a good thing I never had children." She tried for light-hearted but in spite of herself, she could hear the self-pity in her voice. She braced herself for Rose's reaction. Her sister could never stand self-pity.

But Rose surprised her again. "Oh Lord, Kate, they don't come with instruction books, you know. We learn to be parents by parenting. I always thought you would have been a great mother, if your path had taken you in that direction. You have all the right instincts. It's probably what makes you a good chief of police."

Kate's eyebrows rose slightly as she wondered what McKell would think of a chief of police needing the same qualifications as a mother.

A few minutes later, their relationship on the way to being repaired, they hung up with a promise to talk again later in the week. Kate considered calling Amanda but decided it was too soon. The girl hadn't called her since leaving. She clearly wasn't ready to talk.

A knock at the door interrupted her and she called, "Come in."

To her surprise, Trepalli walked in and closed the door behind him. She knew he was on duty today, but he had been avoiding her.

"Chief," he said in greeting.

He looked none the worse for wear for their adventure. Freshly shaven, his thick hair combed back neatly, his uniform looking as if it had just come back from the dry cleaners... No wonder every girl he met fell for him.

"What is it, Constable?" she asked sharply.

He swallowed but looked her in the eye. "Have you heard from Amanda, ma'am?" he asked. "She's not taking my calls."

"And why is that, Constable?" asked Kate, standing up abruptly. "What the hell did you do to my niece that she doesn't want to talk to you?"

Trepalli looked taken aback but he stood his ground. Then his expression faltered and his eyes filled with misery.

"I asked her to marry me," he said softly.

Kate stared at him a moment longer, as her anger slowly drained away.

"Oh, Marco," she said gently. "I'm so sorry."

He nodded. "Thank you, ma'am. Well, if you'll excuse me, I should be on patrol." Without waiting for her answer, he left.

Kate slumped back into her chair, wishing Bert was here.

She closed her eyes, and once again, Sarah Bergstrom's face swam out of the darkness toward her.

THE END

MENDENHALL MYSTERIES SERIES

The Shoeless Kid
The Tuxedoed Man
The Weeping Woman

ABOUT THE AUTHOR

Marcelle Dubé grew up near Montreal. After trying out a number of different provinces—not to mention Belgium—she settled in the Yukon, where people still outnumber carnivores, but not by much. Her short fiction has appeared in a number of magazines and anthologies. Learn more about her at www.marcellemdube.com.

www.ingramcontent.com/pod-product-compliance
Lightning Source LLC
Chambersburg PA
CBHW020332260626
47156CB00004B/1487